BRICK WALLS

by
SIS DEANS

cover art by
NANTZ COMYNS-TOOHEY

A Windswept Book
Windswept House Publishers
Mount Desert, ME 04660

Printed in the United States of America
for the Publisher by
Ellsworth American Printing Services
Ellsworth, Maine 04605

I dedicate this book to my mother for having the love, patience and courage needed to put up with a kid like me.

Special Thanks to:

Wanda Poore Whitten and John Cofran; my husband, daughters; and God.

I.

THE FRAGMENTS COME TOGETHER

Leo shot through the water--arms pulling, legs pumping. Her eyes, raw from the chlorine, followed the thick black line on the bottom of the fifty-meter pool. When the line stopped, she did a flip turn, propelling her small body toward the other end. Back and forth she traced the line, and when her muscles began to burn, she pushed harder. Concentrating on the muffled sounds vibrating through the outdoor pool, she tried to drown out the vivid memory of her mother and Mabel's voices. But it was useless, their conversation followed like the trail of broken water behind her.

That morning she'd been hiding in the pantry when she'd heard her name. Her first reaction was to hold her breath and wonder what she'd done. Whenever it was Leona instead of Leo, it always meant trouble.

"Leona's only ten years old," her mother had said. "I don't know how to tell her. Or Maggie."

Mabel, their maid, who said she'd never become a Catholic because of the way her charges acted, replied, "Children understand more than we give 'em credit for. Best to come right out with it. You're doing the right thing Mrs. G. You got enough to worry about with his drinking and diabetes and all. You don't need to be worrying 'bout those girls, too."

"Saturday night I really didn't think he'd make it, Mabel. It was the worst diabetic reaction he's ever had. The kids were terrified. And the boys. . . Mark won't even talk to him."

"It turns my blood cold the way he talks to that boy," said Mabel. "And Mark tryin' to fix this place up nice the way he does. Now don't you cry Mrs. G., things are gonna work out fine."

"But Leo's so young . . . "

"It's only for a year. They'll be home one weekend a month and holidays, too. 'Sides, Leo's a tough little thing; she'll do just fine. She's gotten kicked out of two schools already. Maybe this boarding school's gonna be good for her. Straighten her out a bit, clean up that fresh mouth. Lord knows, we've all tried. That one's got a mind of her own. Living with them nuns might rub off on her some."

An explosion of bubbles rocked the water as someone jumped in Leo's path. She treaded water, ready to lace the culprit. Jack surfaced, squirting water between big, white teeth.

"Hey, Leonardo, you trying out for the Olympics, or what?"

"You're lucky it was you," she told him, splashing water in his face, "and it's none of your friggin' business."

She sprinted to the side before he could dunk her and hoisted herself out. Hands on hips, she stared back at her scattered reflection. The shadowed fragments slowly came together as the water settled, and when she stared deeper she could see Jack, all arms and legs, sitting on the bottom. Like her, Jack had a reputation for being a troublemaker, but that wasn't the only reason she liked him.

Leo slammed her racing cap onto the deck and dropped down beside it. The warm concrete felt good against her wet body. Resting her chin on her hands, she kept her eye on Jack. He was the same age as her sister Maggie. But unlike Maggie, he didn't mind Leo hanging around, even let her help with his afternoon paper route and gave her a quarter for it.

Finally, Jack got out of the pool and stretched out on his back beside her. "So what's the matter with you?"

Turning her head, she glanced down at the scars that covered his chest like melted cheese--the result of a cherry bomb meant for a mailbox. He'd let her touch them once. They'd felt rubbery. "My parents are sending me off to some boarding school."

Jack laughed. "Aren't there any schools left around here that'll take you?"

"It ain't that," she told him. "It's 'cause of the Old Man's drinking. Ma don't want me and Maggie around him. Like we don't know about it. Everybody knows, but no one says nothing. He's worst of all; he thinks I'm stupid just 'cause I'm a kid. Yesterday he gave me a ride down here and took a drink at every stop sign on Elizabeth Road. He ain't fooling me, I know what's in that brown paper bag."

"So when did your mother drop the bomb?"

"She didn't. I heard her and Mabel talking about it. Mabel said Ma should send us." Leo traced the rubber line on her racing cap. "Some friend she turned out to be. No wonder she ain't Catholic."

"What about your brothers? Are they sending them off, too?"

"No, Hal, Mark, and Mikey get to stay home 'cause they're boys. Ma told Mabel boys can be subjected to more stuff." She chewed on the corner of her cap, rubber tasting like chlorine. "What's subjected mean, Jack?"

"I don't know," he answered lazily.

"You do too. You know everything. Maggie said if you kept your face out of trouble, you'd get straight A's." Leo stared at the purple scars on the back of Jack's hand. "Tell me, " she pushed.

Jack rolled his head in her direction and squinted from the sun. "I guess it means boys understand things better than girls. Like your father being drunk and stuff."

Leo pondered the information. For as long as she could remember, boys had been treated better, simply because they were boys. It was one of her mother's favorite explanations. Because her brothers were boys, they could use the lawn mower, sleep outside, have seconds at the dinner table. Whenever she asked for seconds, the word glutton always came up.

"It ain't fair," she retorted. "Boys get to do everything. They get to be Altar Boys and play Little League, and be subjected. Hell, I can hit a ball further than half them finks in Little League Six, and I got my own glove, too."

She shut her eyes and listened to the pool sounds mingling in the breeze coming off Dougherty Field. She wished she were a boy. She had always wanted to be one. So much in fact, that when she was little, she used to wear her brothers' underwear, thinking it would make her grow that thing that boys have and girls don't.

"Hey, Bertha!" yelled Mellonhead McDonald. "How about a feel?"

Both Leo and Jack turned to watch Bertha Jennings strut across the diving board, her large breasts bouncing. When she got to the end of the board, she turned, and staring straight at Mellonhead, informed him, "Ya hands ain't big enough!"

Jack snickered and Leo heard him say, "That's the truth."

Leo made a face, then watched Bertha dive into the pool. Once, she'd heard Mellonhead tell Butchy Rice that Bertha was a scag. Leo wasn't sure what it meant, but by the way Bertha walked around the deck, she sort of had an idea. She didn't like Bertha, or the way Jack liked to look at her whenever she got out of the pool.

"That Bertha's a scag."

Jack smiled. "You shouldn't say things unless you know what they mean, Leonardo, it could get you in a lot of trouble."

She didn't argue with him. She told herself she'd look it up in Webster when she got home. Home. The thought of it made her stomach hurt. What if her mother told her tonight?

"Boarding school might be fun, Leo," Jack said, as if reading her worried look.

"How could living with a bunch of nuns be fun? I've never met one I liked, and I've met a lot of them."

"That's a lie, what about your piano teacher, what was her name?"

"Sister Constance. And she don't count 'cause she quit the convent and got married." Leo sighed and laid her cheek against the warm cement. "I bet they don't even have a pool. I won't be able to compete all winter, no A.A.U. swim meets, or Seals practice, neither. Just when I got my fly down to a thirty-four flat for the fifty. I'll never be as good as Don Schollander now."

"They might have a pool," he offered.

"Sure, Jack. You ever see a nun in a bathing suit?"

"Well, tell your mother you don't want to go then," he snapped.

She rolled onto her back and opened her eyes slightly so she could see the rainbows on her eyelashes. "I can't tell her that; she feels bad about sending us. It's 'cause of him. It's all his fault. I hate him."

Once, after her father had given her a licking for something she hadn't done, she'd printed 'I Hate The Old Man' in tiny letters around one of the flowers on her bedroom wallpaper. Whenever she got mad at him she'd go and look at it. It always made her feel better.

"I won't say nothing when she tells me. I'll pretend I'm happy about it. I don't want her to cry or nothing. Maggie will cry though. She bawls about everything. She's still crying about what she didn't get for Christmas last year."

Leo dipped her finger into the puddle created by her dripping hair, then wrote her name on the concrete. "Get any letters?" she asked, knowing he would have told her if he had. Jack's older brother, Nick, was in a place called Vietnam.

Jack avoided her question by asking one of his own. "Did you watch the news last night?"

"I don't watch the news."

"If you had a brother over there you would," he said. "The Marines out of Da Nang killed twenty-five guerrillas."

"Why'd they kill gorillas for, Jack? Is Vietnam in Africa?"

"Not King Kong gorillas, Leo, Viet Cong guerrillas. They're Communist soldiers; that's who we're fighting. Don't you know anything? . . . Aw, forget it, you're too young to understand anyhow."

Leo let it rest. She knew Jack was real touchy about that Vietnam place. She was just glad the Marines weren't killing real gorillas. Besides, she had her own war to worry about, and the enemy

7

lived in the same house she did.

Jack leaned over and looked at the clock. "Come on, it's time to do the route."

Grabbing her cap, Leo headed for the showers, a tunnel with four gushing nozzles. She hugged the slimy wall and slid sideways, dodging the icy needles. The girls' room was empty, so she stopped in front of the mirror to examine her racing suit for bumps. She sighed. Tubs, the fattest boy at the pool, had more than she did. For a second more, she studied the tanned face and brown eyes, the broken front tooth that was chipped in a fist fight and looked like a fang, then she pushed herself away from the mirror and backstroked through the locker room. As she swam past the gross pink stalls that smelled of urine, she briefly thought of checking their walls for new writing. If she had a pen, she would have added something about Bertha, only she wasn't sure if it was spelled with an s or a c.

Leo pulled the faded blue captain's hat down over her twiggy haircut. The only time the cap with its leather visor and gold patch ever left her head was when she was in the pool. Without her hat, a gift from her father, she felt naked.

"Hurry up," said Jack. "I've been waiting for ten minutes."

"What a liar," laughed Leo, hoisting herself up onto the handle bars of Jack's bike. "But you'll never be as good at it as Hal."

The bike lurched forward. She leaned back against Jack's forearms, then closed her eyes, listening to his breathing and the music of the baseball card flapping against the spokes. This was one of her favorite places to be--on Jack's bike, moving fast, her back resting against his strong, thin arms, her bare legs and feet dangling in the air. She never wore shoes in the summer, not if she could get away with it. She hid her sneakers in the bushes near her house because her mother was afraid she would get some kind of worm if she walked around barefoot.

They peddled down Douglas Street, past the brick Waterworks and Victory Village, where she used to steal blueberries from Charlie. She hadn't seen Charlie around all summer and wondered if he was still alive. He was an old man who tinkered in his garden all day. He was deaf and couldn't see well. Once, he'd even been in the yard while she was swiping his berries. He'd been standing by his fence with his back to her and she'd yelled, "Charlie, these berries sure are good!" Thinking about him now, she hoped old Charlie had just moved away.

Jack turned onto Brighton Avenue. The traffic was heavy. "Here come the tracks!" he panted.

Leo prepared herself, and just as they were almost over the last of the bumps, a car passing on the inside lane swerved at them. Jack steered away and lost his balance. Leo flew off the handlebars.

She jumped up quickly, her knee stinging.

"What kind of a moron are you!" she yelled at the driver. "You stupid son of a mother!" She bent down, scooping up a small rock.

"Leo!" Jack grabbed her arm before she could throw it.

She wheeled around and glared at him. "He could have killed us."

"He's out of range," said Jack, his face white. "You'd end up hitting someone else."

Turning, she chucked the rock as far as she could toward the vacant end of the tracks.

"Are you okay?" Jack bent forward to examine her knee. The skin was scraped; beads of blood and tiny bits of sand stuck to the layer underneath.

"Aw, that's nothing, Jack, you should have seen the one I got sliding into home." Squeezing the cut to make the blood flow, she added, "Like the Old Man says, I'll live."

"We'll get you a band-aid at the pharmacy." Jack nodded toward the building on the corner where her brother Hal and his gang usually hung around.

"I don't need a band-aid. Mabel will fix it up when I get home."

"I want you to go home now, then."

"No way! We still got the route to do."

"Here." Jack dug into his pocket and pulled out a quarter. "I'll pay you and you don't even have to help."

She looked at the extended hand with the quarter in its palm, then smacked it. The coin flew into the dirt.

"I don't want your lousy money!" She spun around and started limping toward home.

"Leo!"

She didn't turn back. "I hope he gets run over by a truck," she grumbled. "A big, gosh darn dump truck. He didn't even care I was going away. Probably won't even miss me. A person can't trust nobody. Just like Mabel."

Mabel had said they should send her away. Leo couldn't understand it. She'd always liked Mabel, probably even loved her. Mabel had been the only maid that hadn't quit after a couple of weeks, had, in fact, worked for the family since Leo was four. Over the years, Leo had gotten to know Mabel's family as well. She had a daughter who actually liked black olives, and a brother who picked up their garbage every Monday. They called him Dan Dan The Rubbish Man. He was big and cross-eyed, and when Leo was little he used to scoop her up and throw her into the sky. She could still remember the fear of looking down at him, hoping he would catch the right one. Mabel's other brother could talk like Donald Duck, and her sister, who told fortunes for a living, once said Leo had old eyes that could see into people's souls. Mabel probably said they should send her, thought Leo, just to make her mother feel better.

When Leo stopped for her sneakers at her usual

hiding place they weren't there. Twice she crawled around on her sore knee, moving in and out of the bushes, but the P.F. Flyers had disappeared.

Picking up one of the whirlybirds from the maple tree, she spun it with her fingers, thinking hard, the white lie already developing. Her sneakers had gotten swiped down at the pool. She was chasing the thief when she tripped and cut her knee. It sounded good to her, and wasn't that far from the truth--her knee was hurt and her sneakers were gone--God couldn't count it as a whole lie.

Slowly, she walked toward the biggest house on Cragie Street where a sprinkler waved across the tended lawn, flower beds, and trimmed hedges. Her brother Mark did all the garden work and wouldn't let them play on the grass. They had the best looking yard on the street, but never got to use it. At a slug's pace she trudged up the back steps and opened the screen door to the kitchen, letting it slam behind her.

Mabel was at the sink, soap bubbles clinging to her fat arms. "How many times I gotta tell you kids not to let that door slam? Lord, I hear that sound in my sleep, I do."

Leo slid over to the counter before Mabel had a chance to turn around, and climbed up on one of the red bar stools. "Sorry, I forgot. What's for supper?"

She stood up on the bottom rung of her stool, toes curling around the cold metal, and peeked over the lip that separated the counter from the built-in range. On the stove a big pot burped steam. She sniffed, deciding it didn't smell like anything she would want to eat.

Mabel left the sink, moving toward the pot with a wooden spoon. "Got to be some of my best," she said after sampling the broth.

"What is it?" Leo asked, worried. Mabel was always cooking stuff she hated, like spinach, peas, and other green things.

"Beef stew." Mabel closed her eyes, breathing deep, inhaling the vapors.

Leo slumped down onto the stool. "I wasn't hungry anyways."

Her brown eyes snapping, Mabel slammed her spoon down. "You kids don't appreciate nothin'. Cook all day and I'll bet my bottom dollar you'll sneak a peanut butter and jelly when no one's looking."

Leo hopped off the stool and rolled her eyes. The starving babies in India will be next, she thought.

"All those starving babies in India and you turn your nose up at Mabel's best stew ever."

Ignoring Mabel's comment, Leo settled into the chair by the window, and looking over at the Cyzinski's house, felt a stab of envy. The big Cadillac was gone. Every summer the Cyzinski's rented a camp on Sebago Lake for two weeks. It seemed strange not seeing one of the kids out there, the windows of their kitchen so empty.

The Cyzinski's had a color T.V., a tree house, a motorized go-cart, and a mother who wore shorts outside in the summer. Cindy Cyzinski was a year younger than Leo, and went to public school even though she was Catholic. Both of Cindy's parents were big, and Leo thought if a person didn't know them, they might seem mean because they yelled a lot. But she knew it wasn't real yelling; it was just that they talked loud. Mabel had told her all Polish people talked that way, and for a long time Leo thought Father McBrady was Polish even though her brother Hal swore he was Irish.

She gazed at the empty driveway. She missed their yelling, but she didn't miss the way they were always kissing, hugging, and saying they loved each other. Cindy would be standing there and her sister would come up and hug her for no reason at all. It wouldn't even be her birthday or anything. Leo couldn't fathom anyone in her family doing that. It wasn't normal. They all loved each other, but she would be more comfortable with a good shoe fight than if Maggie or Hal told her they loved her out loud. That kissing and hugging stuff was okay for Cindy's family, she figured, because it was sort of like their yelling; something Polish people did, but normal families like hers, didn't.

I wonder if Mr. Cyzinski locked the bulkhead, thought Leo, still studying their house. The Cyzinski's were always forgetting to lock it when they took off for the beach or when they went to see the race horses, and she'd gotten into the habit of watching their color T.V. when they were gone. She wasn't the only one in her family who did that. Once, she'd walked in on Hal making a ham sandwich in the Cyzinski's kitchen. They always had good stuff to eat.

"Are you sick?" asked Mabel. "You're too quiet." She left the stove and walked over to Leo, placing a plump hand on her forehead. "You're not warm."

"Huh?" asked Leo, scraping away a dot of mustard stuck on the arm of her chair.

"Whenever you kids are this quiet, you're either sick or in trouble." Mabel checked her over and quickly spotted the dried blood on Leo's leg. "Lord, what'd you do there?"

Leo felt her face heat up, the rehearsed lie already on her lips. "I was down the pool and a kid, a big one with blue shorts, swiped my sneakers. I was chasing him and tripped over a curb and fell down."

Mabel gave her a strange look. "What kind of fib you trying to get away with? Your sneakers are in the hall, right where you threw them."

"Oh." Leo stared down at her knee to avoid Mabel's stare. "Must have been someone else's. Sure looked like mine."

"You keep on and we'll need a steam shovel to dig you out." Mabel shook her head, trying not to smile. "Now go get me the iodine before I give you what-for."

Leo slid out of the chair and hurried from the kitchen, automatically heading for the back stairs-- her most dependable escape route. Whenever her father chased after her for something she'd done, she would run up the front stairs and down the back ones until he either caught her or was too tired to continue. She figured every house should have two stairways just for that reason. Depending on how much trouble she'd gotten into, he sometimes called in the troops, offering a reward to anyone who caught her. She would bomb up the front stairs with her father on her heels and come flying down the back ones only to find Maggie and Hal waiting at the bottom with dollar signs in their eyes. Mikey and Mark never took part. Mikey was too little and it wasn't in Mark's nature to cause bad feelings, even for money.

Midway up the steps, she hesitated just long enough to inspect the hole in the wall. The month before, during one of her father's diabetic reactions, he'd put his fist through it. He'd told her mother he'd thought the devil was chasing him.

She went up to her room and looked at the flower, traced the letters with her finger, then went into her closet to hide. She had no intention of bringing Mabel the iodine. She knew their maid always left at five o'clock to catch the bus. She would just wait until Mabel was gone. Leaning against the cold plaster wall, she stretched her legs over the heap of clothes that lived in the bottom of her closet and tried to forget. But even in the only place in the house that was really hers, she could find no comfort.

All summer the house had been alive with whispers--hushed tones sliding down the stairwells, creeping along the halls, settling into the dusty corners of its seventeen rooms. She'd hidden in different places, quiet as a cat, straining to hear the words in the whispers, but had only caught fragments. All around her, the air had been electric; something was happening; something was up; but no one was talking out loud. Now the fragments had come together--they were sending her away.

II.

SUPPER AND THINGS PAST

"There's the brat now," Maggie said, as Leo entered the kitchen. "Mabel was looking for you all over. You're going to get it when Dad comes home."

"H-how c-come?" Six-year-old Mikey put his elbows on the counter and stared at them with huge blue eyes.

Leo looked at her little brother, feeling her throat tighten. She could tell he was scared for her. Mikey didn't talk much. Her mother said he had four brothers and sisters to do his talking for him. But Leo knew the real reason--he stuttered.

Mikey's blonde head rested on one of his small hands. "H-how c-c-come?" he asked again.

"Because she's in *big trouble*," Maggie said smugly.

Glaring at her sister, who had boobs, liked nice clothes, and was always curling her shoulder length hair, Leo was tempted to tell her what she'd overheard that morning in the pantry. She knew that would make Maggie howl. "Don't listen to her," Leo finally said. "She don't know nothing."

Leo turned her attention to Mark, standing on the other side of the counter, meticulously dishing out steaming bowls of stew. It was a familiar scene. Their parents never ate with them except for Sundays, and the responsibility of dishing out supper was Mark's. At seventeen, he was the oldest, and the only one their mother could rely on.

Mark's slender hands placed a bowl in front of Mikey. "It's hot," he warned, "make sure you blow on it." Then he ladled up a bowl for Leo.

Leo poked at the stew with her spoon, her appetite deflating as soon as she spotted the peas and carrots.

Hal, who looked older than Mark, but was two years younger, sat down beside her. With pretend reverence, he folded his hands and bowed his head. "God is good, God is great. You'd better grab it fast or there's nothing on your plate."

Maggie laughed; even Mark smiled, but Leo just played with the big chunks of meat, wondering if ketchup would help.

"What's the matter, little sister?" Hal asked her, his lips curling at the corners, his blue eyes dancing. "You dreaming about Jack?"

"No, she's dreaming about getting a training bra," said Maggie.

"Don't worry, Leo, they'll grow." Hal tilted his head back and let out a laugh.

"Better shut up, Hal," threatened Leo, "or I'll

tell them what you told Jean The Dream on the phone last night."

Hal acted like it didn't faze him. "Who cares what I told that maggot."

Maggie leaned toward her. "What'd he say?"

"We're talking at least a quarter," Leo informed her.

"You say a word and you're dead meat." Hal flicked a pea at her. "And if I catch you listening in on the other phone again, you won't live to tell about it."

Mark sat down beside Maggie, unfolding his napkin with piano fingers. "Can't even have a meal around here without you guys acting like a bunch of animals."

"They are, aren't they? agreed Hal. "Pigs, oink, oink."

Maggie caught Hal in the arm with a fist and Hal was about to retaliate with a nuggie when they heard the front door close and smelled his cherry tobacco drifting through the hall.

"Here comes the Old Man," whispered Leo. Both Mark and Maggie got up and put their bowls in the sink. Leo noticed Mark's was still full. As her sister and brother escaped through the pantry, Hal whispered after them, "Run, Totto, run!"

Their father, a man of small build and dark looks, entered the silent kitchen with his shirt sleeves rolled to the elbow.

"H-hi, D-Dad."

Out of the corner of her eye, Leo watched her father's claw-shaped hand pat Mikey on the head.

"Oh, hi Dad," said Hal, acting surprised. "I didn't hear you come in. Would you like me to get you some stew?"

"No, I'll eat with your mother, thanks."

Leo peeked at Hal, wanting to laugh. Hal could get away with that phony stuff. Old women and aunts loved him. On Mrs. Beecher's birthday, he'd told her she didn't look a day over fifty. Mrs. Beecher's daughter had acted like it was the nicest thing anyone had ever said about her deaf mother who had just turned eighty. Hal was the only person Leo knew who could lie straight out and have everyone act like it was special.

"W-want to p-play ch-checkers?" Mikey asked.

"Maybe later," their father answered.

Poor Mikey, thought Leo. She knew when her father said 'Maybe later', it always meant never.

"So how'd work go?" Hal laid it on. "A hard day?"

Her father hesitated by the counter, and Leo watched him lay his driving glasses down on the white Formica. When they were younger, they used to hide his glasses and wait until he offered a reward, then whoever hid them would miraculously find them and collect a nickel or a dime or even a quarter if they held out long enough.

"How much do you need, Hal?" asked their father.

Hal almost spit out his milk. "Gee, Dad," he said, with a look of injured innocence, "I wasn't going to ask you for any money. But now that you mention it, I could use a little."

Leo waited for him to tell Hal 'if you didn't hang out on a street corner all day, you might have a dollar to your name,' but her father didn't say it this time. He just took out the black wallet that lived in his hip pocket and dropped three one dollar bills on the counter.

"Don't spend it all in the same place," he told Hal.

Hal stared at the money. "Thanks, Dad. It will be hard not to."

"What was that?"

"I said, I'll try not to."

"That's what I thought you said."

Leo figured it would be a good time to hit her father up for an allowance while he still had his wallet out, but he'd given her some money the day before and she knew he wouldn't forget. Sometimes he forgot their names, but he never forgot an allowance. Besides, she didn't want anything from him.

She watched him close the wallet with his crippled hands. Often, she wondered what it was like having fingers so stiff they couldn't bend and hardly wiggle. She'd noticed people were reluctant to shake his hand. It always made her embarrassed for him. She slid off her stool and headed for the back stairs, telling herself she wouldn't feel sorry for him anymore. He didn't deserve it.

"Leona."

Her father's voice froze her feet to the linoleum. "Yes?"

"Your bowl."

Putting a healthy distance between herself and her father, she placed her bowl in the sink, then hurried off before he could say anything else.

Pushing herself through the open doorway of her mother's room, Leo asked, "Can I go to the pool for evening swim?"

Her mother, sitting up in bed, looked away from the book she was reading. "Is your father home?"

Leo glanced around her favorite room in the house. It was full of pink and white and sunshine, and crowded with books, their embroidered markers hanging out like colored tongues. "Yeah, he's downstairs. Can I go? I got my own money."

"How's your knee? Mabel said you fell and scraped it."

"It's nothing, just a scratch."

Her mother leaned over. "Let me see."

Quickly, Leo pulled up the pant leg covering her uninjured knee. "See?" she said, yanking it back down. "You can't even see it. So can I go, Ma? Can I? I'll clean my room tomorrow."

Her mother smiled. Her blue eyes were the same warm color as the house dress she was wearing. "Let me see your other leg, Leona."

Leo grimaced. Her mother knew everything. "Would you like me to bring you up some stew?"

"Stop trying to change the subject."

"But if I show you, you won't let me go."

Her mother gave her the 'I mean business' look. Leo reluctantly pulled up the other pant leg and waited for her mother to tell her to go soak it. Whenever any of them got a cut or a sprained finger or similar injuries, their mother would tell them to soak it in warm water. *Go soak it* had become a family saying. "I could soak it in the pool, " Leo offered. "Chlorine is good for cuts."

"You've been down at that pool enough for one day. Now go get me the iodine and band-aids."

Leo groaned and headed for her mother's bathroom. Once inside, she ran her finger along the frosted glass shower. Her parent's bedrooms were connected by a bathroom and the kids weren't supposed to use it. It was done in yellow tile, was big, bright, and, because the kids didn't use it, clean. When her parents used to go out on Saturday nights, she, Hal, and Maggie would get out the binoculars and put a chair in front of the bathroom window. From there they could see into the Cyzinski's kitchen. Mrs. Cyzinski used to give Raymond baths in the kitchen sink when he was little and it had been a big deal getting to see him naked. Now her parents never went out, and Raymond was too big to fit in the sink.

She got the things her mother had asked for and returned to the bedroom. Sitting on the edge of the bed, she watched her mother's white hands and listened to her hum. She'd been a nurse before she'd married, and Leo sometimes tried to picture her wearing a white uniform and working with Dr. Kildare. But it was hard to see her as anything but her mother. Now, feeling her tender hands working out the dirt in her knee, she wondered--how can I leave her? How can she send me away?

"You're quiet."

Leo looked down at her and shrugged.

"Do you feel okay?" Her mother leaned back and placed a palm against Leo's forehead. "You're not hot. Is something bothering you?"

"No." Leo took off her captain's hat, scratched her head, then replaced it.

"There," her mother said, then added, "Are you sure there's nothing the matter?"

Leo looked into her mother's concerned eyes, then quickly away. "Yeah, I'm sure."

A knock startled them. Her father stood in the doorway. For a long moment the room was still; even the curtains over the maple nightstand hung quiet in the evening air. Leo watched her parents exchange looks and decided it was either about his drinking or money. She got up and limped across the braided rug.

"Thanks, Ma," she said.

Her father turned sideways so Leo could pass and she caught a whiff of that familiar smell. He hasn't even had supper yet, she thought. I hate him.

Flopping down on her unmade bed, Leo heaved a big sigh, then kicked off the covers, pressing her face against the cool sheet. Mabel wasn't supposed to clean their rooms; their mother said that was their job, but Leo figured it was a waste of time to make a bed unless company was coming.

She grabbed her orange Cousin It and hugged the stuffed animal to her. Touching the bulging eyeballs, she decided she would take him with her if she had to go to that boarding school. She then looked around the room at the other things she'd take. Her Illya Kuryarkin picture; she couldn't leave without that. Or the one of the Sacred Heart of Jesus. Her mother had given it to her for her eighth birthday. She'd wanted to be a nun then, had even gone around the house with a towel on her head trying to act holy, but she'd changed her mind about being a nun when she'd gotten Sister Luke as a third grade teacher.

There had been something bad about that nun, even if she had worn rosary beads and black robes. She'd seen it in Sister's eyes whenever the nun rapped knuckles with the iron ruler. There was something strange about the way her mouth twitched--like she enjoyed it. Early on in the year, she decided not to do any work for Sister Luke. She melted crayons on the radiator; watched the fish tank; jumped up and ran for the window whenever she heard a fire truck or police siren. She got into the habit of dumping her papers in the sewer; got straight F's on every report card; and it was rare if a school day went by without her feeling that iron ruler. Her mother couldn't understand why she was reading *Charlotte's Web* at home and flunking Dick and Puff in school, and had asked her time and again what the problem was. But she knew she couldn't tell her parents she hated Sister Luke, that she was a bad nun. How could she, when her father told the nuns to give his kids a clout if they had it coming. Besides, everyone knew nuns were holy; they wouldn't have believed her.

She smacked Cousin It, wondering if old Sister Luke was still a nun. Someday, somehow, she'd get back at her. And she wouldn't take the picture of the Sacred Heart of Jesus either--they would have enough holy things at that place.

She heard the lawn mower start up, and rolled over on her stomach, resting her chin on the windowsill. The scent of cut grass rose up to her as Mark maneuvered the red machine around the circular flower bed, his tee shirt hanging out of his back pocket, wagging like a tail. Her mother always said Mark was her serious one. He got straight A's in school and rarely caused any trouble. Leo wished she was like him; then she'd know what it was like to be good and have all the relatives say nice things about her. If she were like Mark her mother would never send her away, no matter how much her father drank or how many diabetic reactions he had.

Out of all of them, her mother depended on Mark the most, and Leo felt this was why her father liked him the least. It seemed to her that the more Mark helped out and the harder he tried to make things look nice around the house, the more her father got after him. He was always on her brother's back about being an Interior Decorator and a Momma's Boy. Unlike her, Mark never defended himself. Whenever their father started in on him,

Mark would go to his room or rake the lawn like crazy, and for days afterward, he would storm around the house like the White Tornado. Whenever Mark was in one of his "cleaning moods," as Hal called them, Leo kept out of his way.

She watched her brother skillfully move the lawn mower around the oak tree. This summer things between him and her father had gotten worse. She wasn't sure if it was because her father was drinking more or because Mark had started to talk back. After Mark had charged some paint to do the front porch, her father, while he was out of it, had written a sign on a piece of cardboard and hung it on Mark's bedroom door. The sign was addressed to the *Third Floor Resident*, and though she couldn't recall all of it, she couldn't forget the part about, *once you turn 18 Buster, you can find another house to paint.*

For two weeks Mark wouldn't talk to anyone, then one night, in the kitchen, her father brought up the paint business again. This time, instead of raking the lawn, Mark stood up to him, told him he didn't appreciate a thing he did around there and he was sick of it. Their father pinned him against the wall, and Leo grabbed her father's free fist, trying to stop the blows, yelling all the while, "Leave him alone!" Hal finally came to the rescue. He was bigger than her father and used to fighting with his gang. Hal grabbed him from behind, and hauled him off of Mark, saying, "It's okay Dad, calm down." Storming out of the room, Mark picked up a mustard jar from the table and winged it in their father's direction. The jar smashed against the wall, sending a yellow rain all over the room. Their father threatened to call the police and have Mark arrested, but Hal talked him out of it.

Hal could always talk her father out of things, or into things. If she wanted something, she knew her chances were better if Hal asked for her. He treated Hal like he was his best buddy. Whenever Hal got into trouble her father said he was just sowing his wild oats. If it had been Mark, it would have been a different story. Although Hal never lifted a finger around the house and acted like putting his plate in the sink was a big deal, he was the only one who could handle their father when he was drunk. He knew the right things to say, could make everything into a joke. She'd watched him do it hundreds of times, had even tried to copy him, but it never worked. Instead of making things better, she made them worse.

She'd also tried doing what Maggie did: ignore him totally. Maggie walked around the house like she was the only kid in the family. The way she talked to her friends, you would think she lived with Leave It To Beaver's family. She pretended nothing ever happened. It bugged her that Maggie could remember getting her tonsils out when she was six, but couldn't recall the fist fight over the can of paint. When she'd mentioned it to her, Maggie had told her she was crazy, that it had never happened, that she was just making it up. She wished she could be like Maggie, wished she could forget as easily as Maggie could. But she couldn't.

When Maggie was ten, their father, by mistake, hit her over the head with the buckle end of his belt. He'd been chasing her up the stairs for something she'd done, and had tried to whack her with his belt as she ran. She'd had to get three stitches. It had shaken him up good because after that he'd started treating her like a guest, like she was someone else's kid. Once, when she told Maggie that was the reason her father never picked on her, Maggie told her she was crazy, that she'd gotten those stitches when she'd fallen down the stairs.

But Leo couldn't hold it in like Mark, or handle him like Hal, or pretend he wasn't like he was, like Maggie. Her temper wouldn't let her. When she was mad at him she couldn't stop the words from coming out of her mouth, couldn't hold it back, even when she heard that snapping sound of leather whipping through his belt loops. Maggie blamed her for getting him started, said she made things worse by wisecracking. She knew her sister was right, but she couldn't help it. Whenever any of them got in a fight with him, somehow she got in the middle of it. She couldn't stand by and watch.

What drove her crazy was how after everything was all over, he'd come and apologize. Whenever he said he was sorry, all her anger seemed to melt away, and she would feel guilty for the way she had acted, and end up feeling sorry for him.

She turned her head toward the wall and ran her finger along the sentence hidden in the wallpaper. Her mother was right about his diabetic reactions, thought Leo, like his drinking, they were getting worse. Saturday, he hadn't eaten or taken his insulin and because of it, he had the worst reaction she could remember. Usually, he would just lie on the couch swearing and getting clammy and they would give him orange juice mixed with sugar until he came out of it. Or sometimes, if he was really bad or in a coma, they'd give him an injection of glucagon. Everyone in the family knew how to give the shot, even Mikey.

But Saturday night was different. He was up and moving around like a scary movie mad man-- stumbling about the upstairs hall, slurring swear words, his eyes looking as though they weighed ten pounds. She and Maggie hid behind their dresser, listening to him stagger into the bathroom, meowing like a cat, a deep scratchy howl. But when she heard her mother trying to talk to him, she came out of hiding and stood in the doorway, afraid he might do something, might hit her mother, though he never had before.

But then, there he was, coming at her. He was bare chested, his pants wrinkled; there was a wild look in his eyes. Maggie hauled her into their room and slammed the door. Together they leaned against it as he tried to push it open, Maggie screaming, "No, Dad, No!"

She pushed against the door until her palms burned, knowing if he got in, something bad would happen . . . something really bad.

He finally gave up and wandered back into the center of the hall. Maggie wanted to push the dresser in front of the door, but Leo told her they had to get Mikey. The thought of him alone in his room had made her forget her own safety. Holding her breath, she crept out of their room. The upstairs hall seemed huge. Her father was on his hands and knees in the middle of it, groaning, making noises. Her mother was on the upstairs phone, and motioned for her to get back. But she ignored the warning and slipped past her father. She found Mikey under his bed, his hands clamped over his ears. He was shivering. She dragged him out, picked him up and ran back to her room. She wasn't sure how she'd managed to carry him, but at the time, he'd seemed light.

By then, Mark and Hal were in the hall trying to help, but they were unable to hold her father down long enough for her mother to give him the shot. For the first time she could remember, Dr. Forest had to come to give the glucagon. It took four medics to hold her father while Dr. Forest injected him. She watched at a safe distance while her father moaned and thrashed out at the arms that held him. Then she retreated to the darkness of her room, huddling with Maggie and Mikey as they listened to the jumbled voices just outside the door. After everyone had left and the house grew quiet, she and Mikey crawled into Maggie's bed. Her sister was crying soundlessly, her body shaking. She held onto Maggie until the windows got light.

The day after, her father cornered her in the den and asked what he'd done, what he'd said. She'd lied, said she was sleeping, but he knew she hadn't been, she could see it in his eyes. He didn't confront her, just said he was sorry if he'd scared her. She'd felt bad for him because he'd said he was sorry.

Recalling the terror of that night had caused goose bumps to spread over her bare arms like a rash, and her fingers searched frantically for a blanket. Night had fallen, bringing with its blackness a cool breeze that turned the leaves on the maples into waving hands. She tugged the blanket up around her shoulders, and in the dim light cast by the portico below, she watched the oak tree's shadow dance across the lawn.

III.

GOODBYE, HELLO

The first Sunday in September the temperature reached eighty by noon. Leo and Maggie's luggage squatted in the sun by the front walk--two large suitcases and a trunk upon which sat Cousin It.

Maggie was on the phone, where she'd been all morning, calling friends, saying good-bye. Leo sat in the shade of the lilac bushes waiting for their grandmother's red Volkswagen. Memere was going to take them to the boarding school. Their mother, who didn't drive, had thought it best if their father didn't bring them. Leo was relieved by the decision. Lately, her father was acting stranger than usual. He walked around the house like he didn't know which room to go in, as if he didn't live there anymore. The past two weeks he'd been really quiet, hadn't even bawled out Hal when he'd come home at one in the morning. He also kept trying to get her alone, but she'd gotten out of it every time. She knew he just wanted to tell her he was sorry about the boarding school, and she didn't want to hear it. This time "I'm sorry" wouldn't work. This time it wouldn't make things all better.

Mikey came and crouched down beside her. Ever since their mother had told them the news about boarding school, Mikey had followed Leo everywhere but the bathroom.

"W-what you s-sitting h-here for?" he asked her.

"'Cause."

"Oh," he replied, as if that were reason enough.

Leo watched as he drew in the dirt with his finger, his blonde head tilted downward. She tore a leaf off the bush and shredded it. She didn't want to leave Mikey. He needed her. She was the only one who paid any attention to him. Half the time no one even knew where he was, and if one of them did ask, the usual answer was: "I don't know, look for him. He's got to be around here somewhere." But when their father was home, they knew where to find Mikey. Mikey hung around him like a begging dog: his checker board always ready, waiting for "maybe later" to come. If their father needed his slippers or the paper, Mikey was right there to get it. What amazed her was that he didn't seem to mind. He acted like fetching things for their father was the most important thing he had to do. There was no doubt about it, out of all of them, Mikey loved him the most.

Leo's stomach felt as tight as it did before a race. She'd give anything to dive into a pool right now. She reached down and touched Mikey's hand.

His blue eyes looked up at her and he let out a big sigh. The kids called him Mental Mikey because he threw temper tantrums. He'd gotten straight A's last year in first grade, but that hadn't stopped the teasing, only made it worse--they called him teacher's pet as well. Once, she'd beaten up Billy Ramus because he'd yelled "M-Mental M-Mikey," in the schoolyard. Now she wouldn't be around to take care of jerks like Billy.

Leo saw the red Volkswagen turn down the street and jumped as if something furry had touched her.

"W-w-what's the m-matter?" Mikey asked, jumping too.

"Memere's here."

"You got t-to g-go n-ow?"

"Hello, Leo! Hello, Mikey!" called their grandmother in her heavy French accent. "It's hot, no?"

Leo and Mikey ran to Memere and let her hug and kiss them without protest. "Where's your mother and father?" she asked them. "Inside?"

Leo looked at her grandmother. She wore a white dress with bright red buttons, and her straw hat sprouted a red feather. Memere was a hat lover, too. Leo tugged her captain's hat down over her eyes. "Ma's in her room."

Mikey took a deep breath, trying not to stutter. "My dad w-went for a ride. He's n-not back yet."

"Listen to you! He's doing good, eh Leo? And so handsome! Like a prince. Better than a prince." Memere gave Mikey a squeeze, then spotting the luggage, said, "All that in my little car? Maybe you'll have to ride on the roof, eh, Leo?"

"It's all Maggie's stuff," Leo told her. "Only one suitcase is mine."

Mark and Hal joined them and made a project of fitting all the baggage into the car. One large case ended up in the back seat. Leo took off her hat and fanned herself, watching Hal crush the rest of the luggage into the trunk.

She looked down the street, hoping to see her father's car. She'd at least wanted to say good-bye.

Maggie and their mother came out of the house-- Maggie was all puffy-eyed. Leo could feel the tension. This was it. Time to go.

"Oh, they're going to have so much fun at the school," Memere said, consoling Mikey, who'd begun to cry. "Did you know I went there when I was a girl? And your mother and her sisters, too. Eh Cheri?"

Their mother nodded, her lips quivering into a smile. Mikey buried his face in the folds of her house dress and she ran her hands through his hair.

"You've done a nice job on the lawn, Mark," Memere said, changing the subject. "You work hard for your mother."

Mark smiled shyly, fidgeting with his hands.

"What about me?" asked Hal, puffing up his chest like a bird.

"You, Halley, are too handsome for your own good." Memere laughed, then, taking him aside, told him, "You take care of your mother; she needs your help."

He nodded. "I do, don't worry."

"Come on girls!" Memere called. "I got to get back to the farm and make Pepere's supper. You know what a bear he is."

Leo laughed despite what she was feeling. Her Pepere was kind and gentle, a big man whose laugh could rattle plates and whose hands could make any plant grow.

Hal coughed. Mark shuffled his feet. Leo couldn't stand there any longer. She might run away, or worse, cry. She gave her mother a quick hug, then bent down and whispered to Mikey. "I'll write you, okay?" She kissed him, then crawled into the back seat and laid on top of the suitcase.

Maggie, still crying, finally got in the front seat while their mother held onto the door, speaking softly of visits, letters, phone calls. Her mother shut the door, then walked around to Leo's side. "You be good, Leo," she said. "And here, this is just for you."

Leo reached out her hand and her mother pressed a neatly folded twenty dollar bill into her palm. Leo looked down at it and thought of Jack and how he'd tried to buy her off that day on the tracks. "I don't need it," Leo told her.

"Keep it, sweetie," said her mother, "you might."

She watched her mother back away, walk to where her brothers were calling out : "Have fun! . . . Don't forget to write! . . .You'll be home in no time!"

· Her grandmother started up the car. Maggie hung out the window, sobbing, waving. As the car pulled away from the curb, Leo turned and looked at

her big white house with its black shutters; the
columns holding the portico; the oak tree; her
brothers waving; and her mother standing in her
light blue shift, looking, watching, until the car
drove down the hill and out of sight. Then she
rolled over on her back, the suitcase hard beneath
her, and shut her eyes, squeezing that last image into
a memory.

As they drove down Brighton Avenue, Leo
peered out the window at Hal's gang, killing time on
the drug store's corner. They were known as the
Pharmacy Boys. Whenever she walked by their turf,
they always treated her nice, always said hello and
never made fun of her like she'd seen them do to
other girls. She knew it was because everyone liked
Hal. Besides, with his reputation as a fighter, they
would be crazy to treat her any other way. Being
Hal's sister had gotten her out of more than one
scrape.

She looked past them to that spot on the
sidewalk where the bundle of newspapers were
usually waiting for her and Jack. If it were a
weekday, she might have seen Jack on his way to do
the route. She hadn't helped deliver papers since the
pool closed, and had never really had a chance to
say good-bye. The last time she'd helped him, he'd
been in a bad mood because he hadn't gotten a letter

from his brother in a while. He always carried Nick's latest letter in his back pocket. Once, he even let her read one. It was as shiny as a magazine cover and coming apart at the folds; full of stuff about brothers and doing good in school.

"Are you comfortable, Leo?" asked Memere, stopping for a red light.

Leo met her grandmother's eyes in the rear view. "Never rode on a suitcase before."

"You're a good girl. And Maggie, too. You're helping your mother more than you know."

The mention of her mother brought a salty sting to Leo's eyes. The week before she'd taken her and Maggie uptown on the bus. She bought them new underwear, nightgowns, socks, and some white shirts to go with their jumper uniforms. They ate lunch at the Village Cafe, and her mother said they could order anything they wanted. Maggie had lobster; Leo, a hot dog. Their mother never took them out for lunch--it had been a special deal.

It took almost an hour to get to South Benton, and Maggie sniffled the whole way. When Memere finally said, "This is the exit," Leo almost started sniffling herself. She wanted to get out of the cramped car, wanted home, summer, wanted to dive in the pool and follow the black line until her eyes burned.

"This is it?" asked Maggie, as they drove down the biggest street in South Benton.

Leo stared at the empty sidewalks, at the handful of men standing in the lot of the fire station, and at the only store in sight: Fred's Hardware. Like

Maggie, she wondered where the city was.

"Isn't it a pretty little town?" asked Memere, but Leo and Maggie didn't answer.

Memere made a left-hand turn, and it was then that Leo saw it. The front part of the school facing Main Street was white clapboard; the rest, which extended a good distance down a side road, all brick. She looked at the brick walls, three stories high, and despite the heat, shivered. Rows of windows glared down at her, reflecting the sun. A large white statue of the Blessed Mother, its arms outstretched as though waiting for a hug, stood beside a black sign with gold lettering: Academy of St. Mary's.

The driveway to the school was circular and wound its way around the building. On one side, a huge playing field stretched out like an airport runway. The car came to a halt and Memere pointed toward a modern metal building that to Leo looked like a huge tuna can.

"That's the new gymnasium. They didn't have it in my day or your mother's. Isn't it nice you have a place to play?"

"Does it have a pool?" Leo asked. She'd packed her racing suit and cap just in case.

"I don't know," answered Memere. "We'll have to find out."

Memere drove slowly around the driveway, then parked in back of a station wagon. Leo leaned forward, staring at a crowd of girls. They were hugging and jumping up and down like the kids on her team did after someone broke a record.

She looked up at a porch that ran almost the

entire length of one side of the building. Girls were sitting, some with family, some alone, in green wooden patio chairs. But the girl who drew her attention immediately was leaning on the white railing. She was black. Leo had never seen a Negro, except for on T.V. or in her mother's *National Geographics.* Billy Ramus' father said it was too cold for them to live in Maine. She studied the girl, wondering what it would be like to live with one. Then she spotted two other girls who were different. They were dark, but not Negroes. She knew she'd seen their nationality in a magazine or book but couldn't come up with it.

Memere got out of the car and Maggie looked back at Leo. "Can you tell I've been crying?" she asked.

Maggie's face was blotchy, her eyes red, like she'd been swimming in the pool all day. "No," Leo told her, "I can't tell."

After the confining ride, when at last she could get out and move her legs, Leo didn't want to. But Memere was already hauling out their luggage--she didn't have a choice. Once out of the car, she did a couple of knee bends and, arching her stiff back, stretched her arms, yawning loudly. She noticed everyone was looking at her and Maggie--checking them out. Maggie acted busy with the luggage, trying to ignore it, but Leo pushed her hat up slightly, put her hands on her hips, and stared back. Her eyes kept settling on the black girl. I wonder if she's Catholic, thought Leo. All the people who went to St. Patrick's were white.

"Come on, girls," said Memere.

Leo went first, strutting up the stairs as though she'd lived there all her life. When she got to the top, she halted in front of the black girl. Maggie, right behind her, lugging an over-packed suitcase, walked on Leo's heels.

"Get moving," whispered Maggie.

But Leo stood a second longer looking at the black face, dark eyes, full lips. "Are you Catholic?" she finally asked.

The girl almost knocked her over with her laugh. "What's the matter, honey? Haven't you ever seen a black Catholic before?"

"No," Leo told her. "I've never seen a Negro in real life, neither. Billy Ramus' father says it's too cold for you to live in Maine."

"Oh, God," groaned Maggie.

The big girl laughed again. "Girl, Catholics come in all colors. And I like the cold."

Leo smiled at her, then continued on as if she'd just asked the time.

"She doesn't know any better," Maggie tried to explain. "We don't let her out much."

"At least she's honest," the girl replied, then as an afterthought asked, "Would you like me to show you to the office?"

"Thank you," said Memere. "Everything has changed so much since I was here last. I'm all turned around."

By the time Memere, Maggie, and the girl, who told them her name was Evette, hauled the suitcases through the door, Leo had already scoped out the rec hall. The room was huge. It had a high white ceiling, a wooden floor, a piano, a record player, and to Leo's relief, a T.V. There was even a small enclosure that housed a snack bar and store. Maybe living here won't be that bad, she thought.

Leaving their baggage behind in the rec hall, they followed Evette down a corridor lined with classrooms. "These rooms are for the high school students," Evette said, then turning to Maggie inquired, "Are you a freshman?"

Maggie nodded.

"I'm in fifth grade," said Leo. "Had to go to summer school once so I didn't stay back."

"You'll be going to St. Christopher's, then," Evette told her. "It's that building on the other side of the parking lot. That's where the graders have classes. You'll like it there--they have boys."

Leo was glad to hear that. The last school she'd gone to was all girls and she'd been bored to death.

"I think you're the only grader this year," Evette continued.

"What's a grader?" asked Leo.

"There are three kinds of students here," Evette explained. "The upperclassmen are juniors and seniors; the lower classmen, freshmen and sopho-mores; anyone below that's a grader."

Maggie smirked at Leo. "You're as low as it gets."

"Who cares," said Leo. "At least I get to go to school with boys."

Evette stopped in front of an opened door and knocked softly on the frame. "Excuse me, Sister St.

Paul, but these new girls just arrived."

"Come it! Come in!" called a husky voice.

Leo stepped through the doorway and instinctively found a wall to lean against. She watched Memere cross the tiny room and vigorously shake the nun's hand.

"Mrs. Lajoie?" asked the nun.

Memere nodded. "It's a pleasure to meet you, Sister St. Paul."

"Thank you, I've been looking forward to the girls' arrival. I've had such lovely letters from their mother."

"She wished she could have come. She loved this school when she was a girl," said Memere, still holding the nun's hand.

"It's becoming a tradition for your family."

"Ah, yes, Sister, and someday for my great-grandchildren, too. Such a nice school for the girls, St. Mary's."

Leo watched the nun carefully. She was short, trim, wore the new habit: a patch of black hair showing just in front of her veil. Leo inspected the narrow face; the brown eyes behind wire-rimmed glasses; the front teeth, crossed slightly at the tips. When she'd heard the nun's voice in the hall, she'd expected someone much larger.

"That's all, Evette, thank you. You may go now."

"Yes, Sister."

"She's a very nice girl," said Memere.

Sister smiled, then motioned for Memere to sit. "Please, make yourself comfortable. I'm sorry I can't offer you girls a chair. As you see, there is very little space."

"That's okay," Leo said, "I've been laying on a suitcase for an hour."

"I have a Volkswagen," Memere explained.

Sister laughed. "You must be Leona. I've heard a lot about you."

"From who?" Leo asked, worriedly, "Sister Luke?"

"Well, we did get your records, but I was referring to your mother."

That's good, thought Leo. Her mother would never write anything bad about her. She stared at the nun, still not trusting her, discomforted by all her smiling. She figured she was probably acting so nice because Memere was there--all teachers knew that trick.

"Let me tell you a little bit about the school, then we'll get you girls settled." Sister cleared her throat. "The Academy Of St. Mary's has an impeccable reputation. Our aim is to mold our girls both spiritually and intellectually . . ."

Leo thought the nun sounded like she was reading from a book, but Sister was staring straight at them.

". . .Our students are from many backgrounds. We have girls from El Salvador, Mexico, Canada, New York, all over. Some are learning English for the first time. This blend of cultures makes for a colorful environment, an excellent learning exper- ience . . ."

Leo gave up listening. She was hot, thirsty, felt

closed in. She focused on the back of her grandmother's head, at the gray hair peeking out beneath the white hat. She felt a painful twinge at the thought of Memere leaving them there. She loved her grandmother. No matter how much trouble any of them got into, Memere always found a good reason for it.

". . . the girls' day begins at five-thirty. Mass is promptly at six. Breakfast follows. At seven-fifteen, chores are carried out. Each girl is assigned a certain job to perform for the year. It may consist of dusting the dorm, or sweeping the stairs, just a small task. After chores, school begins. Classes end at three, and after thirty minutes of free time, first study hall begins. Supper. . ."

Leo rolled her eyes at Maggie.

The nun caught the look and paused. "I know it's been a trying day for you, and this is a lot to digest, especially since you just arrived. I think it would be better if your dorm nun, Sister Theresa, went over your schedule with you later."

"It has been a hard day for them," Memere agreed.

"I'll escort you back to the rec hall and see if I can locate Sister Theresa. She'll help the girls get settled. Do you have any questions before we go, Mrs. Lajoie?"

Memere shook her head. "None I can think of."

"I've got one," said Leo. "I want to know if you have a pool in that tuna can building."

Sister forced a smile. "I believe you are referring to our new gymnasium. No, Leona, we

47

don't have a swimming pool, but we do have a beautiful basketball court."

Some luck, thought Leo; wait until I write to Jack.

"Isn't she nice?" asked Memere after Sister St. Paul left them in the rec hall.

Leo didn't answer but agreed with Maggie's whisper, "I wouldn't trust her as far as I could throw her."

While they waited for their dorm nun to arrive, Memere bought Leo and Maggie a treat at the snack bar. Leo got a 3 Musketeers and a soda, wolfing down both on the spot. Maggie got chips, and Leo kept waiting for her to open them up so she could ask for dibs.

"Aren't you hungry, Maggie?" asked Memere.

"I'm going to save them for later," Maggie answered.

Figures, thought Leo. Maggie was always like that with food; her Halloween candy lasted until Easter.

"Hello."

Leo turned and watched an exceptionally tall nun amble toward them. The nun's eyes were too small for the flat, freckled face, and the first thing that popped into Leo's head was the scarecrow on the Wizard of Oz.

"I'm sorry to keep you waiting. Sister St. Paul

just caught up with me. A lot of confusion here today." She reached down her hand for Memere to shake. "I'm Sister Theresa, the girls' dorm nun."

"I'm their grandmother," said Memere. "It's nice to meet you."

"My pleasure," said the nun, then she leaned down and gave Leo's visor a little tug. "So this is the one I've heard so much about."

Leo took a step backward, wondering if there were any nuns in this place who hadn't heard about her.

"And you must be Margaret," said Sister Theresa, turning her attention to Maggie. "What pretty girls."

"And smart," said Memere. "You wait and see how smart they are."

"I'm sure," the nun agreed. She draped an arm on Maggie's shoulder. "Well, I think it's time I take them to the dorm and get them settled. I'm sorry, but we feel it's best if parents and relatives leave before we take them up. It makes things a little easier on everyone."

"I understand," said Memere. "I have to get back myself, anyway."

A minute later, they were standing outside, hugging and kissing their grandmother good-bye. When Memere finally got in the car, Leo could no longer look at her. She stared at the ground, at the bits of silvery sand embedded in the tar, hoping for a miracle: that Memere wouldn't leave them there.

Maggie walked toward the car as their grandmother backed out, then stood waving, crying hard. When Memere beeped her horn, Leo finally looked up, catching just a flash of red as the Volkswagen disappeared around the corner.

When the nun's hand touched her shoulder, Leo jerked away.

"It's all right to cry, dear," Sister Theresa said softly.

Maggie wiped her eyes and sniffed loudly. "She never cries. Even when you hit her."

The dorm reminded Leo of a church hall with beds in it. A partial wall, as tall as she, divided the room in two. On either side of it was a row of twenty or more beds, each separated by a tiny dresser and a small wooden chair. Windows, too high to see out of, ran the entire length of the right side of the room.

She looked up at the ceiling that seemed higher than the one downstairs. It was white with a pattern of fancy leaves along the edges. From it hung fluorescent lights, and she found herself thinking they'd have to use one heck of a tall ladder to change the bulbs.

"Keep coming, girls. You've been assigned the last two beds in this row."

Leo watched Maggie and the nun struggle down the aisle, the trunk swaying between them, but didn't follow. Instead, she walked over to the row of four sinks and tried to look in the mirror above it. But even on tiptoe, she couldn't see. "Great. Everything in this lousy place is made for the Jolly Green Giant."

She left the sinks to explore the bathrooms. There were three, with a tub and toilet crowded into each.

"Come on, Leona."

Leo heard Sister call, but took her time, flushing each toilet to see if it worked. Satisfied, she retrieved her suitcase and started walking to where Maggie and Sister Theresa were unpacking. It was then that she noticed the cubicles on the left. Each one had three walls with a curtain in front, and contained a bed, dresser, lamp, and a chair.

"Hey, I want to sleep in one of these," she told Sister Theresa. "They're nicer."

Sister smiled. "Those alcoves are already taken, dear. Besides, there's an extra charge for them."

Leo shrugged, then looked at the pile of clothes on Maggie's bed. "No way you'll get all that stuff in that dinky thing," she said, pointing at the dresser.

"She's right, but you'll each have a locker down in the basement where you can store your extra things," Sister told them. "When we're done here, I'll show it to you."

Leo sat on her bed, bounced a few times, then laid down and declared, "At least the toilets work." She rolled over and looked down the row of beds, some made up, some still bare, then sat up and watched with interest as Sister St. Paul walked in. The nun showed a girl about Maggie's age, and the girl's mother, an alcove directly across from her bed.

"When you said private, I assumed you meant a private room." The pretentious woman stood back and examined the alcove, her hand delicately placed over her mouth.

"I'm sorry if you misunderstood," said Sister St. Paul. "Only the seniors have private rooms."

"Well, Hope," the woman said to her daughter, "I suppose you'll just have to bear it."

"You said I'd have my own room, Mother."

"I can't help that. For the extra expense, I'd expected you to have more than a curtain for heaven's sake."

The girl, who was tall, stocky, and had pretty long blonde hair, tapped her foot madly. "It isn't fair, Mother. You told me I'd have my own room."

I'll trade with you, thought Leo.

"Why don't I show you the rest of the school," Sister St. Paul said pleasantly.

The woman glanced at her watch. "We'll have to make it short. I have a flight to catch."

Sister nodded. "We'll hurry right along."

After the three had left, Leo jumped off her bed and asked Sister Theresa, "How come her mother got to come up here? She special or something?"

"Some things are hard to explain, Leona," Sister said reverently, then changed the subject. "The top drawer is for underwear and socks. The second drawer, sweaters, third drawer, blouses . . ."

Later that night, after the lights were out, Leo lay in her new bed, her stomach growling. Supper had consisted of spinach, some kind of meat she couldn't name, and watery mashed potatoes that slid around on her plate. In the cafeteria, she and Maggie had sat by themselves, the other girls' summer chatter buzzing about them like mosquitoes. Maggie played with her food as if it were something important, and kept demanding under her breath that Leo stop staring at Evette. But Leo couldn't help it: the black girl fascinated her.

Her empty stomach growled again and she repositioned Cousin It. The bed, even the sheets, were stiffer than hers at home. She closed her eyes and listened to the sighs, the sniffing. From almost every bed came the sound of crying. In her mind, she brought back the memory: her big white house with black shutters; her mother in her blue shift, waving; her brothers standing on the lawn. The only one missing from the picture: her father. Her body felt as stiff as the bed, her muscles rigid. He hadn't even been home to say good-bye.

A crackling noise broke into her reverie and she concentrated on the sound of cellophane being torn apart. In the large room with its endless ceiling it sounded like eggs frying in a hot pan. She looked over at Maggie and, in the dim light from the driveway below, she could see her sister eating potato chips.

"Psst. Gimme one."

"Only if you'll sleep with me," Maggie whispered back.

"I want two then."

Leo slipped quietly into Maggie's bed and together they ate the rest of the chips, sucking on each one until they were soft enough to chew without making noise.

"Blow up the bag and pop it," Leo told her when the chips were gone.

"Sure, you heard what Sister Theresa said about food in the dorm. They'd probably kick us out."

"That's the idea, stupid."

Maggie put the bag out of Leo's reach. "Go to sleep."

"How can I? Everyone in here's bawling their eyes out."

Maggie moved closer to her, and Leo could feel her sister's breath against her hair as she whispered, "He could have been home."

Leo curled herself against Maggie's warm body. "Yeah," she sighed. "He could of."

IV.

ENEMIES AND FRIENDS

After a blasting bell penetrated the school with two, long, shrilling rings, the lights in the dorm flashed on. "All rise! Chapel in fifteen minutes!"

Her ears still vibrating from the jarring sound that had woken her, Leo squinted in Sister Theresa's direction, and remembered with disappointment where she was.

"What a way to wake somebody up," she told Maggie as they untangled their arms and legs.

"Leona," said the nun, stepping toward them.

"Yes, Sister?" Leo asked, wondering if Sister Theresa had heard her.

"I'm sorry, but from now on, you must sleep in your own bed. It's a rule."

After Sister Theresa was out of earshot, Leo whispered to Maggie, "She says 'I'm sorry' an awful lot."

During mass, Leo watched the older nuns in traditional habits massage their beads; lips silently moving in prayer. She figured some of them were old enough to be dead and wondered how long they'd lived there. Hal had told her the only reason a woman became a nun was because she was too ugly to find a husband, but she didn't believe it. She thought anyone who didn't mind getting up for mass every day of their lives had to be holy and looks had nothing to do with it. She glanced over at the younger nuns, dressed in modern habits. She figured they'd end up looking like the wrinkled ones, and wondered if it bothered them.

On the altar, the priest held up the host, his red and gold vestments shimmering in the soft light of the chapel. Father Richie was tall, thin, balding even though he was young. His eyes--magnified behind thick glasses--were milky blue, distorted, almost dead looking. He took a white handkerchief and, for the tenth time, Leo watched him wipe his nose.

"I hope Old Fish Eyes ain't the only one who says mass around here," she whispered to Maggie.

Maggie ignored her, and Leo turned her attention back to the priest who was kissing the chalice. When she was little and wanted to be a priest, she'd practiced in their playroom with Kool Aide and Oreo cookies. The memory made her stomach rumble.

"Shhh!" Maggie hissed, looking holier than thou.

"I can't help it," Leo told her. "I'm starving after that crap they gave us for supper."

The girl on the other side of Leo muffled a laugh behind her prayer book. Leo had heard someone call her Calsa and thought it was a neat name. Beneath a white chapel veil, Calsa's black hair stuck out wildly. Her thin face, with its hooked nose, seemed lost in it. She tried not to stare at Calsa's arm, but her eyes kept going back to it. The arm was tiny, shriveled, and hung across her stomach as though it were broken. When their eyes met, Calsa smiled at her as if to say "it's okay to look." Feeling a rush of guilt, Leo turned away, pretending to be interested in the stained glass windows.

The pictures of Christ and Saints done in reds, blues, and darker colored glass, peered down at her as if they knew what she was thinking. Beneath them stood the heavy wooden doors to the confessional. During her First Confession, Sister Jude had stood with her ear to the door, making sure all the kids said their Act Of Contrition right. Thomas Stuper had a bad stutter like Mikey, and the kids used to call him Tommy Stttupid. He'd said his Act Of Contrition wrong, and Sister Jude had swung the door open, dragged him out by the hair and had given him a good shaking. Leo had watched, terrified, yet curious as to how Sister Jude could get such a good grip on Tommy's crew cut. When it had been her turn to go into that dark box, she'd said her

Act Of Contrition in a whisper. She'd stood on the kneeler and stuck her lips against the mesh screen, hoping Sister Jude couldn't hear in case she blew it like Tommy.

The thought of confession caused her hands to feel sticky. Every Saturday afternoon her mother made them all go, and Leo thought it was expected to confess sins even if they hadn't been committed. While waiting her turn to go into the tiny enclosure that smelled of old bodies and varnished wood, she'd sit in the pew and make up her list of sins. She always put a number in front of each one, and would end each confession with, "I told one lie." The latter sin, she felt, would cover the confession she'd just made up.

The whole idea of confession was still a mystery to her, one she never questioned but accepted as part of being Catholic. She had, however, learned a few tricks about it from Hal: never go in after an old lady because their perfume would suffocate you and always get in line behind a kid because they would be in and out in no time.

The nuns filed out in a single line, hands folded, tongues ready for the white wafers. Leo decided she'd go to Communion even though, with their leaving, she and Maggie hadn't gone to confession that week. She knew hunger was no reason to accept the body of Christ, but figured he'd understand. Stepping out of the pew, she fell in line behind Calsa and, as she waited her turn, she thought about her brothers. She wondered if they were up yet, if they were eating breakfast, if they missed her as much as she already missed them.

"Body Of Christ."

"Amen."   She sucked down on the wafer--
somewhere along the line someone had told her it
was a sin to chew the host and she'd always been
careful not to. She returned to the pew and, kneeling
down, bent her head to pray. "Dear Jesus, bless my
family, even the Old Man, and I hope you're not mad
I took communion, Amen. P.S. Please let breakfast
be better than supper. Amen, again."

Breakfast: oatmeal, toast, poached eggs. Leo
was on her third piece of toast smeared with waxy
peanut butter when Sister Theresa came over to her.

"How's your breakfast, Leona?"

Leo looked down at the untouched eggs and
oatmeal. "I bet they're having pancakes and syrup at
home. We always do on the first day of school."

"That's a new one," said Maggie.

"She don't remember anything important," Leo
explained.

"And you remember things that never happened."

"Do not."

"Do so."

"Okay, girls, let's not argue about it." Sister
placed her hand on Leo's chair. "When you're done,
Leona, I want you to come with me. I want to
introduce you to Sister Alphonse. She's going to
show you what to do for a chore."

"What about me?" asked Maggie.
"Check the list on the bulletin board for your name.
I think you've been assigned to our dorm. Dust

mopping the floor, I believe."

When Sister left, Maggie pushed her tray away and mumbled, "They should have a Mabel for doing that."

"I bet Hal's on his second plate of pancakes by now," Leo said wistfully.

"Shut up, will you." Maggie shot her a dirty look. "We have to start at a new school where we don't know anyone and all you think about's your stomach."

"So what? Besides, what's the big deal about a new school? They're all the same." Leo tore her napkin into shreds, watching the table across from them where three of the Mexican students sat. She liked their pierced ears, dark looks, and the rat-tat-tat-tat sound of their language.

"Well, maybe if I'd gotten kicked out of as many schools as you have," Maggie continued, "I wouldn't think it was such a big deal."

"I wasn't kicked out," Leo said defensively. "You know Ma don't like you to say that, or expelled, neither." Leo returned her attention to the Mexicans, but added, "They just thought I'd do better somewhere else. That's what Ma says."

"It means the same thing, you idiot. Think Ma's going to go around telling people you got kicked out of two Catholic schools? It's embarrassing."

"Hal got kicked out of one them, too, and nobody made a big deal about that."

Hal was the only one in the family who went to public school. He'd been expelled from Cheverus for sneaking beer into a dance.

"That was different," Maggie said with authority.

"No it wasn't," Leo countered. "Nobody said anything 'cause he's a boy and 'cause no matter what he does, the Old Man says he's just sowing his wild oats. Aw, what do you know anyway. You can't even remember how you got your stitches."

After depositing her tray with the others, Leo followed Sister Theresa to the basement where a tiny old nun was waiting for them. As Leo and Sister Theresa approached, the nun vigorously nodded her head and smiled. She looks like a mole, thought Leo, staring at the nun who had no chin, puffed cheeks, and squinty eyes.

"Sister Alphonse," Sister Theresa said loudly, "this is the little girl I told you about."

The old nun, her head still bobbing, reached out and patted Leo's hand. "Good, good. I show her what to do." The nun turned slightly and waved at Leo to follow her. "Dis way, dis way."

Leo looked up at Sister Theresa, "Do I have to?"

"There's nothing to be afraid of, Leona. Go ahead. She'll show you what to do. When you're done, go right over to St. Christopher's."

Sister Alphonse waved again. "Vient! Vient!"

Leo followed the scurrying nun. Sister Alphonse walked hunched over, as if she had a big rock on her back, but it didn't seem to interfere with her quick pace, and Leo found herself running just to keep up with her.

They went through a narrow tunnel in the basement, then into a room off it. The room was small, its concrete walls painted steel gray. Buckets, mops, and other cleaning materials were neatly lined up against a wall. By the door, there was a tiny metal desk with a crucifix hanging above it. Leo thought the cross, with the outstretched body of Christ, palms and feet dotted with red, didn't belong in a room with mops and no windows. She glanced around the dingy place, wondering what her job would be, yet afraid to ask.

She watched carefully as Sister retrieved a huge cardboard box from the corner. The nun dragged it over to where Leo was standing and patting it, told her, "Dis box. You take dis box and empty all de trash cans."

Leo looked down at the box in disbelief. "In the whole school?"

The nun grabbed Leo's arm with her knobby fingers, her squinting eyes, inches from Leo's face. "Ven you speak, look at me. I watch you lips, no?" The nun let go and touched the ears beneath her veil. "No good, no more. They give me a . . ." Unable to find the English word, Sister Alphonse made a small O with her fingers. "A thing to wear, no? I don like it." She gently patted her mouth. "I watch your lips." The nun smiled, exposing tiny yellow teeth. "Ven all done come back, okay? You do dorms, classrooms, come back. Bathrooms, too."

"Sure, if you say so."

"Don tell Sister Theresa I no wear my thing, okay?"

"Okay."

"You a good girl. Now go, go. You late, they mad at me."

Leo hurried out of the room, the cardboard box bouncing off the back of her heels. She was glad to be out of that place; glad to be out of reach of that little nun.

Dragging the huge box, she started on the third floor, emptying the wastebaskets in the sophomore and junior dorms--army green metal cans full of hard Kleenex balls, hair, toothpaste boxes, and other throw away things. On the same floor as her dorm were the seniors' private rooms. She liked emptying their trash. All their rooms were fixed up in different ways: posters, bright scatter rugs, wastebaskets brought from home--pink ones, yellow ones, flowered ones. She felt like she was meeting the girls themselves just by how their rooms were decorated and what was in their trash. In one room she found a wrinkled drawing of a horse, in another, the basket was full of Hershey Bar wrappers, and in yet another, she found a perfectly good pen which she put in the pocket of her uniform. By the time she got to her dorm, she was thinking it wasn't such a bad job after all. She'd already found a pen, a broken red pencil sharpener, and an Archie comic book.

"Oh, my god!" Maggie stood next to one of the beds with a dusting mop. "Where'd you get that box?" She pointed and started laughing. "What do they have you doing!"

Leo looked at the box that said Kotex on the side in big black letters. "I'm Dan Dan The Rubbish Man."

Maggie, who had a weak bladder, held onto herself and laughed harder.

"What's so funny?"

"The box!" Maggie, now hysterical. "The box!"

Leo was starting to get irritated. "What's the matter with it?"

Maggie dropped her mop, held onto herself with both hands.

Confused, Leo watched her sister run for the bathroom, then shrugged it off and continued on.

After doing the dorms, she did the classrooms. The laboratory was the last room she entered, and was entirely different from the rest. It had black counters all around, with tiny built-in sinks and microscopes. But what caught her attention was the smell--a sweet, wet smell, like in the pet store at Monument Square.

Calsa stood in front of a metal rack singing, 'I Want To Hold Your Hand', while cleaning rodent cages with her good arm.

"Wow! Whose rabbits?" asked Leo, leaving her box at the door and quickly crossing the room.

Calsa turned. "Hi there cutie. What's happening?"

"Can I pick one up?"

"Sure, why not? Watch out for the back feet

though."

Leo lifted out the smallest white rabbit and peered into its frightened red eyes. "I sure wish I had this job," she said, then gently patted the soft fur, feeling the rabbit tremble. She looked up at Calsa, then at her little arm. "How do you pick them up?"

"You mean because of my arm?"

Leo nodded. "Were you born that way? I never seen anyone with a little arm like that before. Does it work?"

Calsa let loose a dry cackle. "It works some. I just can't pick my nose with it."

Both girls turned at the noise in the doorway. Sister St. Paul had tripped and half fallen into the large Kotex box full of trash.

"Leona!" snapped the nun, standing up with difficulty. "What do you think you're doing?" Sister St. Paul stood rigid, her face turning red. "Do you know what time it is?"

Time to get out of here, thought Leo.

"You have exactly five minutes until chores are over and you're going to be late. Late because you're dawdling in here." The nun glared at Calsa. "And I hold you responsible, Calsa. You know the rules. I can see you're starting this year off the same way as last." Then she looked back at Leo. "We run an efficient ship around here, Leona, and it's best you learn right off that time is not wasted. Now take that box down to Sister Alphonse this minute. And don't leave it where someone can trip over it again." Sister St. Paul wheeled around and strode out the door.

Leo, still bewildered, looked at Calsa. "What's the matter with her?"

Calsa took the rabbit from Leo's arms and put him back in the cage. "Oh, don't worry about her, she's always like that on the first day. She isn't bad once she knows you."

"I don't know," said Leo, "usually when people get to know me, they like me worse."

Back in the tunnel, Leo followed Sister Alphonse up a bulkhead that led to the outside. The nun dragged the cardboard box across a dirt path to a large metal incinerator with a cinder-block chimney. There, she showed Leo how to clean out the ashes using a small shovel and metal pail. Then the two of them lifted the box, dumping the rubbish into the small oven door.

"All done. Dat's all you do. I make the fire later afda I pick up trash in our place."

Leo knew she meant where the older nuns lived. Sister Theresa said they called that part of the building the Mother House, and that students weren't allowed to go in there.

"You a good worker." The nun rattled off some French and patted Leo's back. "Good girl. Go to school now. I see you tomorrow. Same thing, no?"

"Oui, Sister. Au revoir," said Leo, using the only French she knew besides the swear words.

The nun let out a ripple of laughter, clapping her hands and nodding her head in delight. "Au revoir, my Petite Chapeau."

Like the Academy, the outside of St. Christopher's Grammar School was all brick. Leo stood on the edge of its playground, watching the townies arrive in their new back-to-school clothes. How come they don't have to wear uniforms, she wondered, as she tugged at her Academy jumper, feeling even more out of place.

She'd meant it when she'd told Maggie schools were all the same, but, still, she never liked the first day, the first week, when everyone would stare at her because she was new. Now they'd have another reason to stare at her: her uniform.

When the bell rang, she lined up with the fifth graders, looking at no one, holding onto her new binder until her knuckles turned white. She thought about the new pencil case inside it, with its good smelling erasers and different colored pencils, then felt a jab of pain. Her mother had bought it for her that day they went for lunch.

Her classroom was like any other she'd been in. There were five rows of connected wooden desks with empty ink wells and initials engraved on their tops; a flag in the corner; and there, above the blackboard, the picture of the Sacred Heart Of Jesus. Just like I figured, she thought.

As the kids filed in, Leo went straight for a window seat. A boy who looked much older than the rest, sat across from her, smiling. He had a crew cut and big, mossy green teeth that stuck straight out of his mouth and hung over his bottom lip. His clothes were mismatched, his belt so long it almost wrapped around his skinny body twice.

In back of her sat a girl with her hair in a ponytail. When Leo smiled at her, the girl gave her a snooty look, then asked, "Got nose trouble?"

Leo turned her back on her, regretting she'd bothered to smile.

"Good morning class."

Everyone stood. "Good morning Sister Marie."

Leo numbly moved her lips through the Pledge of Allegiance and morning prayer, dreading that moment when she would be introduced--all the schools she'd gone to did that to the new kid.

"Leona, please stand. And remove your hat in class, please."

Here it comes, she told herself. She stepped out into the aisle and removed her hat.

"Class, Leona is our newest member. She comes from Portland and will be living at the Academy. Everyone give her a big hello."

"Hello, Leona," the voices sing-songed.

Leo sat down, her face hot with embarrassment.

"From Portland, well la-de-da," whined the girl behind her, and two girls sitting in the next aisle giggled.

Leo pretended not to hear, but the words circled in her mind all through Religion and Math. When the bell for recess finally rang, she bolted to the door. She had to get outside so she could breath-- this being the new kid stuff never got easier.

In the schoolyard, Angie, the girl with the

ponytail, started in on her.

"Think you're pretty cool with that hat, don'tcha?"

"You talking to me?" Leo asked, pointing to herself.

"No, the invisible man," said Angie, and the two girls flanking her started laughing.

Leo tried to pass it off as a joke, but Angie wouldn't leave her alone. She grabbed Leo's hat and started playing pass with her two friends, while taunting Leo with stinging phrases--"Betcha can't get it, Convent Girl . . . Betcha can't get it, Fang Face!"

One thing led to another and before Leo knew it, she'd given Angie a bloody nose. She'd expected Angie to give up--they usually did--but Angie didn't and they wrestled to the ground. Sister Marie finally broke it up and they were both marched away. Their punishment: a week of detention.

Leo went through the rest of the day quietly, harboring hate, sinking into herself, her thoughts at the pool, swimming, watching the black line. After detention, she returned to the Academy and was quickly tracked down by Sister St. Paul.

"Into my office. Immediately!" said the nun, walking past her.

Leo followed, watching the nun march ahead like one of the men on Gomer Pyle.

"You know why I called you in here, don't you?" asked Sister, taking a seat behind her desk.

Leo stared at a blue cup full of pencils, trying to think of a place to put her hands. "I got an idea."

"Don't be sarcastic, Leona. And look at me

when I'm talking to you."

She looked up at the nun's black eyes--she had seen them before--on her mother's fox fur. She used to have nightmares about it: the fox would chase her around the house and just as she was about to jump on up on the counter, the fox would bite into her ankle.

"I understand you were expelled from your last school for fighting. Well, young lady, let me inform you, it will not be tolerated here, either."

Leo felt something tighten in her stomach and rested her hands there.

"Now, tell me what this was all about."

"I don't know."

"You don't know! You give a girl a bloody nose for no reason?" Sister's face turned the same shade as the red notebook on the desk. "Who started it?"

Leo tried to swallow, but her throat was dry. "Does it matter?"

"Yes, it does!" Sister pounded her fist on the desk as if to drive home the point. "What happened?"

Leo looked at her, stared into the angry eyes, then beyond her, to home with its white columns and her mother in her blue shift standing by the oak tree, arm raised.

"Answer me!"

Then she was in the pool, racing, doing the fly, her hips rocking, arms pulling, her lungs waiting for that next breath.

"Leona!"

Leo came back to the room, to the nun. "I ain't

got nothing to say."

"All right," Sister told her, tapping a ruler against the desk. "But let me warn you, Leona, I've dealt with your kind before. You won't get away with that insolent behavior around my school. And I won't have my girls involved in brawls in the schoolyard or anywhere else for that matter. Is that clear?"

"Is that clear" was one of her father's favorite lines after he hit her. "Don't give me any lip," whack, whack, "Is that clear?"

"Leona?"

"Yes, Sister. It's clear."

"Good. You may go now. And Leona--this had better be the last time you come into my office for fighting."

"Yes, Sister."

All week after school she and Angie had to wash blackboards, clap erasers, and shut windows. Leo ignored the girl. Their mutual dislike followed them from room to room like a bad odor. Ever since the fight, Angie and her friends had stayed away. In the schoolyard, she sat on the bench and watched them from a distance, saw them point, snicker, heard the names shot like darts--city slicker, fang, mad hatter. But on their last day of detention, as they waited for Sister Marie to tell them what to do, Angie finally broke the silence.

"I bet you don't even smoke cigarettes," said Angie.

Leo looked up slowly, trying to cover her surprise. "Who doesn't?" she shot back.

"What kind?" Angie challenged.

"Umm, Winstons, what else?"

"You got any?" Angie fixed her with a green-eyed stare.

Leo looked away. "No, they took them away from me."

"I got some." Angie leaned toward Leo. "You wanna smoke one?"

"Here?"

"No, stupid, in the woods."

"When?" asked Leo.

"When we're done, stupid."

"My name's not stupid, it's Leo."

Angie paused. "So, who taught you how to fight . . . Leo?"

Leo turned in her chair so she was facing the girl. "My brother Hal. He can take anyone."

Sister Marie interrupted their conversation and put them to work. The whole time Leo clapped erasers, she kept wondering if Angie had her friends waiting to beat her up. But when they were finished with their detention, she went with Angie anyway to the woods behind the school. Although she'd been ready to put up a good fight if she had to, she was relieved to find Angie's sidekicks weren't hiding in the bushes.

Angie removed a pack of Winstons from her jacket, and shook one out for Leo.

Leo took the cigarette, and sniffed it like she'd once seen a cowboy do in a move. "Smells fresh."

"No kidding," said Angie, looking at her strangely. "What are you gonna do, smell it, or smoke it?"

Angie lit hers up and Leo watched, then monkeyed her. The first puff made her choke.

"Hey, don'tcha even inhale?" asked Angie.

"Sure," Leo lied, "I just don't feel like it today."

"So what's it like living with a bunch of nuns?" Angie asked her, flicking her ashes. "Do they wear black pajamas?"

"It rots. And we never see them in their pajamas." Leo looked down at the cigarette between her fingers--it made her feel grown up, but it tasted lousy--made the inside of her mouth feel like cotton.

"How come you gotta live there?"

"My parents sent me."

Angie blew a cloud of smoke in Leo's direction. "I'd run away first, no kidding." She took another drag, then rubbed her cigarette into the ground. "What's your dad do?" she asked, giving Leo a sharp look. "Are you rich like the rest of 'em over there?"

"I don't know," Leo answered, studying the girl. Angie had worn the same dress all week. It was getting grey around the collar. In class, she'd noticed Angie's shoes were coming apart near the toe, as if her feet were growing out of them.

"My father makes a lot of money," Angie said, haughtily. "He's an engineer in sanitation."

"Wow, that sounds important. My father works for my grandfather. They build stuff, but I don't think he makes a lot of money 'cause whenever one of us kids asks him for some, he says, 'What do you think? Money grows on trees?' Then usually he'll tell us how he had to eat squirrels when he was a kid."

"No kidding? He ate squirrels?"

"That's what he says. He says us kids have the life of Riley."

"Who's Riley?"

"I don't know, but I think he's one of our relatives. We got tons of them."

Angie leaned over and carefully removed Leo's hat. She turned it over in her hands inspecting the black leather visor. "Where'd you get this hat, anyhow?"

"Old Orchard Beach," Leo said wistfully. It was the best day of my life, she thought. "Ever been there? They got a million rides and a Noah's Ark with a buzzer seat and everything. The Old Man bought us all a hat like this. But I'm the only one that wears it."

"The Old Man?"

"That's what we call my father when he's not around." Leo crushed out her cigarette, then stood up. "I'd better get going. If I'm late for study hall they'll probably lock me up or something."

"They really don't do that, do they?"

"You should see the food they make us eat." Leo dug into her book bag, then handed Angie one of her new pencils. "Here, this is for the cigarette."

74

Angie took the gift and inspected it. Leo watched, waiting for her to say they were even. She'd learned long ago that nobody gave you something for nothing, that somewhere down the line you ended up paying them back more. Her father was always saying, "I ask you to do me a favor and you expect three in return." She didn't want to owe Angie any favors.

"Gee, thanks, Leo," Angie finally said, "it's a nice one." Then she shoved the pencil in her pocket.

V.

BURNING ANGER

As the weeks went by, Leo fell into the school's routine. In the month since they'd been there, she'd written to her family almost every day, and each night after "lights out," she would lay in bed thinking of home, wishing she were there. She missed her brothers terribly, and the fact that none of them had written was a constant disappointment. Each morning she would tell herself, "Today I'll get one," but no letters from her brothers ever came.

That her father hadn't written was expected. She didn't want any letters from him. It was easier to be there if she could blame him for it. At night, in the darkness of the dorm, she tried to remember all his broken promises, recalled the fights and the fear, in order to keep her anger alive. But often her memories betrayed her. Instead, she remembered how he would say he was sorry, or how he'd bought her a bike, or how he'd taken them to Old Orchard Beach that time. She didn't want to miss him, but she couldn't help it.

Now, as the sun slid behind the maples and afternoon study hall dragged on, Leo finished rereading her mother's latest letter. Her mother had written to her twice, and both letters had been opened before she'd received them. The nuns read all their incoming and outgoing mail, and it bugged her. She figured they did that so no one would tell their parents what the place was really like or how bad the food was. Even Calsa had told her the food was nothing to write home about.

Carefully, she replaced her mother's letter into its baby-blue envelope. Figures St. Paul would tell her about the fight, she thought. Her and her ship talk. Since that day Sister St. Paul had hauled her into her office, Leo had steered clear of her. Whenever the nun was about, she ducked into bathrooms or doorways. She'd learned the sound of Sister St. Paul's footsteps as keenly as she knew her father's-- she could hear the nun coming a hallway away. Still, Sister occasionally sneaked up on her, and when she did, instead of hello, it was "Your shoe is untied . . . You have hairs on your blazer. . . Pull up your socks. . . Slow down!" Calsa had told her Sister St. Paul's father was a Captain in the Navy and that was where she got all those queer sayings like, "Inspection at 0800! . . . I want this place ship-shape in all quarters!" The next time she tells me to pull up my socks, thought Leo, I'll tell her to walk the plank.

Leo looked down at the baby-blue envelope: when she and Maggie went home for free-weekend, she'd tell her mother her side of the story about the fight with Angie. Besides, it didn't matter now, anyhow. Since that day they'd smoked in the bushes, she and Angie had become best friends. Everyday after school they hid in the small stretch of woods until it was time for her to go to study hall. Their secret time together was the only good part of the day other than visiting the rabbits.

She looked up at the clock, her stomach growling. At home she'd never cared what time it was. Here, time ran her life. It seemed like every second of the day was accounted for. Cripe, I even go the bathroom by the clock now, she thought.

Waiting for the bell to ring, she glanced over at Maggie, who was passing a note to Calsa. She still hadn't figured it out yet: Maggie actually liked the place. Worse than that, she acted like she didn't even miss home that much, although she still bawled about it from time to time. Now that Maggie had all kinds of friends, she wouldn't even eat with her anymore. I don't need her either, thought Leo.

When the supper bell finally rang, Sister Bernedette herded them down to the cafeteria, and the whole way Leo prayed for hot dogs. Being small made it easy for her to dart through the moving crowd. It had become a game to see how close to the front of the line she could get. Tonight, she made it to number eleven, beating her previous record of thirteen. Pleased, she pretended to receive a medal for the feat, and when she picked up her plastic tray, gave a brief bow.

"How much?" asked Carin, taking Leo's tray.

Leo looked at the Spanish rice that was mixed with bits of chicken and celery. It looked like maggots in blood sauce. "None."

Carin passed Leo's tray to Marsel, who was standing behind the vegetables. "Stewed tomatoes or green beans?"

"Neither."

The empty tray moved onto the desert. Canned yellow peaches in syrup. "I'll have some of those," Leo told Wendy, then watched the girl dole out the allotted two. "Boy, can you spare it?"

Wendy looked both ways, then added another peach and handed Leo the tray.

"Thanks," Leo told her, "I'll remember you in my will."

She went over to the bread counter and was about to stock up when she sensed someone was watching her. She figured it was someone waiting to get bread, but when she turned around, there stood Sister St. Paul with a puzzled look on her face.

"Are you not feeling well, Leona?"

"I feel okay, Sister."

"Then why aren't you eating?"

The nun's concern threw her off guard. She gave a disgusted shrug in the direction of the Spanish rice, and without thinking, said, "I don't want to eat that crap."

As soon as the words were out, Leo realized what she'd done. She hadn't meant to say it--it just slipped out. "Crap," was her father's word--"I'll beat the living crap out of you" . . . "Don't you give me that crap" . . . "He's full of crap right up to his ears."

79

She hadn't meant to say it--it just slipped out.

The nun slapped her across the face with an open hand, then locked her fingers onto Leo's elbow, dragging her to the front of the line. "Fill up her plate," she commanded.

Carin raised her eyebrows helplessly, and Leo watched as she put a scoop of rice, with its watery sauce and chunks of celery on her tray.

"I said fill it, Carin!" yelled Sister St. Paul.

The girl quickly piled it on, and handed it back to the nun. Everyone watched as she roughly led Leo by the arm to one of the tables in the corner. "No one is to sit at this table," she said to those still standing in line. Then she put the tray down, and pushed Leo into the chair. "You will eat everything on that plate. Do you hear me?"

Leo stared down at the mush, her face still stinging from Sister's slap. It wasn't fair! It wasn't her word!

"You won't leave this room until that plate is clean. Do you hear me?"

She could feel everyone looking at her. Her ears felt hot, her throat dry. She blinked back the tears, her arm still hurting from Sister's tight grip. "I hear you."

The nun turned and started to leave. The other girls stared at their trays in dead silence.

Leo clenched her fists, burning to hit the nun for embarrassing her as he always did, for tricking her as he always did, for punishing her for something he always said. And when the nun was halfway across the cafeteria, she could hold it in no longer.

"I hear you!" she shouted. "But you can't make me eat it!"

Sister St. Paul froze in her tracks and Leo stood up, bracing for retaliation. But Sister didn't even turn around, just marched out of the room.

Leo sank into her chair, frightened by her own defiance, almost regretting what she'd just done, yet feeling relieved by it. It was as if all the anger had been spent, and she felt quiet inside, almost sleepy. She stared at her plate, then pushed it away.

Maggie took her tray over to the condemned table and sat down.

"You better not sit here," Leo told her. "You'll get in trouble."

They stared at each other.

"I'll sit wherever I want," answered Maggie.

Sister Theresa came up behind them. "I'm sorry, you'll have to sit at another table, dear. You heard what Sister St. Paul said."

"Why should I?" demanded Maggie. "She's my sister, and Sister St. Paul didn't have a right to do that. Just because Leo didn't want to eat this garbage. This is America, you know!"

"I think we've had enough scenes for one night, Margaret. Please take your tray to another table."

"Go on, Maggie. I'm okay, now."

Maggie muttered under her breath, then picked up her tray and moved reluctantly.

Leo watched her go, thinking, I love you, too.

"Please start eating, Leona," Sister Theresa told her softly. "You'll only make things worse if you don't." Then the nun walked back to her station.

Leo looked at the Spanish rice. She wouldn't eat it if they paid her a million bucks.

"You told her, Leo," Calsa whispered on her way by, then let out her dry cackle.

Leo turned and smiled. Sister St. Paul didn't like Calsa either. On the demerit chart in the hall, Calsa had more marks next to her name than Leo did.

She took her hat off, shook her hair back, then replaced it, pulling the visor down over her eyes. She could hear her name move around the tables as the girls discussed the incident. To block it out, she tried to concentrate on home. She longed to be there, wanted, at that moment, to feel her mother's arms around her, to hear her say, "It's all right, Leo, it's not your fault."

"Hang in there, kid."

Leo looked up as Doris walked by, then watched her deposit her empty tray on the rack. Doris looked like she weighed as much as Leo's Aunt Bo, and her wastebasket was always full of Hershey Bar wrappers. Calsa said, that next to Evette, Doris was the smartest one in the school.

She rested her head on her arm and glanced around the room at those who were still eating. Her gaze stopped on Hope. Hope always held her fork funny, her little finger sticking straight out like it didn't belong to the rest of her hand. No one liked Hope. Maggie said it was because she was stuck on herself. But Leo could still remember how Hope's mother had acted that first day in the dorm and figured with a mother like that, what did they expect.

Some of it was bound to rub off. Just like her father rubbed off on her. She couldn't help saying "crap," anymore than Hope could help acting like her mother. Besides, she felt sorry for her. Sometimes at night she would hear her crying. Once, she'd even gotten out of bed because of it. But just as she was about to turn Hope's curtain back, she decided maybe Hope liked to cry alone, too, and went back to bed.

"Can't you eat just a little of it, Leo?"

"I'm not hungry," she answered, noting that Sister had called her Leo instead of Leona. Although the nuns weren't supposed to call them by their nicknames, Sister Theresa sometimes forgot.

"I'm sorry, but I can't let you leave until Sister St. Paul says so."

It bugged her that Sister Theresa always tacked, "I'm sorry," onto everything she said. It was like Maggie saying, "you know" all the time. "Don't worry about me, Sister," she told her. "I won't leave. But I ain't going to eat, neither."

"You're a stubborn little girl," sighed the nun.

"That's what my mother says, too, but Memere says it's okay. She says America was built by stubborn people."

A smile flickered on Sister's flat, freckled face and, as she walked away, Leo thought she heard her chuckle.

By then, everyone had left except the scholarship girls who worked in the kitchen. Although she couldn't see them, she could hear them. Listening to their clanging and water sounds as they cleaned up, she felt a burning feeling in her stomach. She was starving. Lunch had been pea soup and shepherds pie and all she'd eaten was bread. When they left, she told herself, she would swipe a couple of slices from the bread box and make an air sandwich.

When the clanging stopped, a handful of girls in pink hair nets emerged from the kitchen. From across the room they waved to her and she waved back.

Evette whispered loudly, "Keep the spirit, Leo!" Then flashed her the O.K. sign.

Leo smiled. Like Hal, Evette could always make her laugh. Evette was from New York City, and Leo liked her accent almost as much as she liked the Mexicans'. For the first few days she'd wondered what it would be like living with someone who was black, but now that she knew Evette, she didn't think of her as being different anymore. Like Calsa, Evette didn't mind if Leo hung around her, and every night Leo saved a seat for her in the T.V. room. The news was the only program allowed, and the only reason she watched it was because Evette did.

As soon as the older girls left, Leo sneaked over to the bread counter and helped herself to a couple of slices. Carefully, she replaced the bag just as she'd found it, in case someone noticed: like Sister St. Paul. She's Sister Luke all over again, thought Leo. If they lived in the same convent, they'd probably be best friends.

Wandering back over to her table, she told the

empty room, "Bet Mabel made her fried chicken tonight. Bet they had corn on the cob and her German chocolate cake, too." Then she pretended she was home in her own kitchen with her mother and all her brothers. The sandwich was now Mabel's fried chicken--"her best ever." It tasted so good, she even ate the crusts.

For the next two hours, Leo waited, and waited, for the sound of those footsteps. Finally, out of boredom, she took the chairs from her table and placed them in a straight line. After sitting down in the first one, she looked over her shoulder and told the invisible passengers, "All aboard! First stop's Portland! Everybody please take a seat . . . Come on Dorothy, and don't forget your little dog, too. There's no place like home. There's no place like . . ."

"What do you think you're doing?"

She hadn't heard her footsteps--there'd been too much noise on the bus. Meeting the nun's stare, she let go to the imaginary steering wheel, but didn't answer.

"Why are you still here?" Then the nun looked down at the full tray, at the fork Leo had stuck upright in the middle of it. "You didn't eat a thing."

Oh, yes I did, Leo told her silently, I had fried chicken and corn on the cob and Mabel's German chocolate cake, too--so put that in your pipe and smoke it!

"Wipe that grin off your face, right now, young lady," Sister warned her. "And go directly to the dorm. Study hall is almost over."

"Yes, Sister," said Leo, then she got up and

walked around the nun, leaving a healthy distance in case Sister tried to hit her again.

At the doorway, she glanced over her shoulder. Sister St. Paul was still staring down at the untouched tray as if it were going to bite her.

"Leo, hurry, you'll be late for chapel."

Leo poked her head out from under the bed. "But Sister Theresa, I can't find my hat. I've checked all over. It ain't anywhere."

"You'll have to look later." Sister said, glancing nervously at her watch.

"Won't you help me? Please? I got to find it."

The nun looked away. "We've got to go. Now, Leona."

"But I can't find my hat." Leo's eyes searched the room. All the other girls had left.

"Get off the floor," Sister snapped, "and go to mass!"

Leo stood slowly. She'd never heard the nun speak that way before. Sister Theresa had always been nice to her. "Are you mad at me?"

The nun closed her eyes. "Leona, just get to chapel."

All through the service Leo hardly noticed Fish Eyes mumbling the mass. She watched Sister Theresa, sensing something was wrong. When mass was over, she skipped breakfast and went up to the dorm to search for her hat. She pulled the sheets off her bed, checked the pillow case, and under all the other beds. She even checked places she knew it wouldn't be.

When the bell rang for chores, she rushed down for her box and did the three floors in record time in order to have a few minutes to look before class. But it wasn't necessary, for when she and Sister Alphonse went to clean the ashes out of the incinerator, she saw the visor that hadn't burned. Sister Alphonse saw it, too. The old nun picked it up from the shovel and stared at it, then at Leo. Sister's mouth hung open in a large O.

Leo felt numb. For a moment, she couldn't move or take her eyes from Sister's hand. Then she reached out and pulled the visor from the twisted fingers, and walked away.

In the courtyard, unshed tears blurred her vision and the morning chill penetrated her light blouse. She passed the gazebo and kept walking until she reached the top of the hill. There she sat, dew soaking into her uniform. She ran her fingers gently over the charred visor. Her father had given it to her. They didn't have any right to take it! They didn't have any right to burn it! It was hers! She remembered how Sister St. Paul had looked at the tray: she was the one. And Sister Theresa--she'd told her to go to chapel, wouldn't help her look-- she'd known. They must have stolen it while she was sleeping. Took it off her head and burned it. But the visor hadn't burned. Leather didn't burn.

She looked at the school, its brick walls blood red against a gray sky. Towering over the trees, the building's narrow windows stared back at her. It was a prison that even looked like the nuns who lived in it--cold, hard, scary. Those nuns who had stripped her of the one thing that was important to her, the one thing that set her apart from all the other uniforms, the only evidence she had of her father's love: her hat.

Anger fed her, soothed the pain, gave her strength. She concentrated on the charred visor in her hand, felt her grip tighten, then she glared at the school through wet lashes. Inside her mind, she was constructing walls of her own. Walls made of a substance stronger than red brick. Walls that wouldn't let anyone hurt her again--not those nuns, not her father, not anyone. They could punish her all they wanted, but they would never be able to hurt her again.

She kissed the visor, then put it in her pocket. She would carry it with her everywhere to show she knew what they had done. And she would never forgive them. Never.

VI.

HOME

Leo handled the hat burning like she'd seen her brother Mark handle things: for a time, she stopped talking. But instead of cleaning the house like he did, she attacked the library with fury. During the five hours of study hall each day, she left Sister St. Paul and St. Mary's behind, escaping into a world of characters and places created by words and imagination. Between the covers of a book no one could touch her--it was a safe place to hide.

To teachers and other students she spoke only when asked a question. Angie was the only one she confided in. Their friendship had become tighter. Angie had dropped her other friends and, at recess, she and Leo hung on the fringes of the schoolyard, talking. She told Angie about her father's drinking and life at home, and Angie told her about her parents' fighting and admitted her father didn't really make much money running the town dump. These shared secrets held them apart from the other kids, and they never had to promise not to tell. It was understood.

On the first Friday in October, Memere came in her red V.W. and collected her and Maggie for free-weekend. The road to Portland seemed to stretch forever. Leo kept staring out the window, waiting for their exit sign, for something familiar. When Memere asked why Leo was so quiet, Maggie answered for her. "She doesn't talk much anymore."

Memere gave Leo a worried look, but didn't ask why.

As soon as they stopped in the driveway, Leo jumped out and raced up the front walk. She moved through the downstairs as if seeing it for the first time, touching objects, searching the rooms for Mabel, Hal, Mark, Mikey. But the rooms were silent, empty. Where was everyone; hadn't they missed her? From behind her she heard Maggie and Memere bringing in the suitcases, and bolted up the stairs, wanting to be the first one to see their mother.

Her mother looked up from her book, a surprised look on her face. "You're home! I didn't expect you this early. I didn't even hear you come in."

Leo stood in the doorway waiting for her heart to stop pounding. "They burned my hat. They stole it off my head when I was sleeping and burned it." She held out the visor for her mother to see.

"Who did?"

"Sister St. Paul and Sister Theresa."

Her mother got up quickly and moved toward her. She tried to hug her, but Leo turned away. "I hate it there. I don't want to go back."

Her mother seemed to deflate with a sigh, and Leo saw her eyes begin to water. "I don't know what to do, Leo," she said. "I just don't know."

"You mean I have to go back?"

There was no answer.

"Fine. See if I care. I didn't miss any of you anyway." Running down the stairs, she almost knocked Maggie over, and when she went out the front door, she slammed it as hard as she could.

She had no thought to where she was going, only felt the need to walk, to get away from the place she'd waited so long to get back to. After seeing what they'd done to her hat, her mother was supposed to say she never had to go back there again, was suppose to say she could stay home for good. Each night before falling asleep she'd pictured herself telling her mother what they'd done. Each time, the way she would say it, varied a little, but always her mother would be shocked, would hug her and say she never had to go back there again. She'd believed it; she'd even told Angie, "You wait until my mother finds out. I'll never have to come back here."

At the pool, she climbed the cyclone fence by the gate and dropped to the concrete deck below. The pool was empty and the black lines on the bottom looked different, flat. She jumped off the side into the shallow end, her hollow footsteps echoing as she skirted the few puddles laying in dips on the uneven bottom. Sitting in the deep end, she leaned against the side of the pool and looked up at the blue walls that seemed part of the sky. She could almost hear the voices of summer, the kids diving off the boards, the sound of the starting gun. She saw herself leave the block, hit the water, arms, legs moving through it, racing on and on, the flip turn, the push off way ahead of the rest. She touches first, looks up at the amazed timers checking their watches. A new record! The crowd in the bleachers clap and stamp their feet. Here she's something! It doesn't matter that her parents aren't there watching-- that they'd only, in fact, gone to one meet--what matters is that she'd won.

She sighed, touching a rust spot beside her. The roar of the crowd was gone. She'd only imagined it, just as she'd imagined her arrival: everyone there to greet her.

"So where you been?" laughed Hal. "Ma said you got pissed off and left. Actually, she didn't say pissed off."

Leo stood in the back hall looking blankly at Hal, who sat on a stool in the kitchen.

Mikey rushed up to her with outstretched arms, and she felt them encircle her waist.

"I-I m-missed you b-bad."

"Good, 'cause no one else did," she mumbled, returning his hug.

"Oh, listen to that," said Hal, standing up. "Nobody loves me, everybody hates me, I'm gonna eat some worms . . ." He gave her a big hug. "Maggie told us about your hat. That nun sounds like a real sweetheart."

"Yeah, she is," Leo responded, then glanced around the room. "Where's Mabel?"

"Up-p stairs." Mikey told her. "Sh-she took me to g-get th-the gr-groceries in her c-car."

"Mabel's got a car?" asked Leo, looking at Hal.

"A real bomb. It's pink." Hal made a face. "Whenever she stops at a light you gotta jump out and put rocks in front of the tires so it doesn't roll away. Mabel says for a hundred bucks you can't expect a limousine.

"W-where you g-going?"

"I'm going to see Mabel."

She found Mabel cleaning the kids' bathroom. She was on her hands and knees, scrubbing the floor. Leo cleared her throat so Mabel would notice her.

"Well, there you are." Mabel leaned back on her heels and swiped at a loose wisp of hair.

"Hi, Mabel. Did you miss me?"

"I thought I did, but now I'm not so sure."

Leo's forehead puckered at the brow. "How come?"

"Because your Momma's in there crying her eyes out on account of you. Telling her you didn't miss her. Telling her you hate that fine school she sent you to. Why, I never met such a selfish child."

"But Mabel," Leo said defensively, "you don't know what it's like there."

Mabel gave her a hard look. "You just be thankful you ain't here, girl. You don't know what

93

that's been like, either. Your Momma's been through hell and back with that man and his drinking. You should be thankful you don't have to see it. Spouting off about how hard you got it. I got a mind to take you over my knee right now. She don't need you making her feel guilty on top of everything else. A woman can only take so much before she breaks." Mabel took a big breath. "There, I said what I wanted. Hand me that brush, will you? And don't step on the floor."

Leo handed her the wooden scrub brush. "I didn't mean to make her feel bad."

"I think you'd better tell her that. She's been walking on eggshells all day waiting for you girls to come home. Had me take Mikey shopping so you'd have your favorite meal for supper." Mabel began scrubbing again. "That woman gives and gives and never gets back."

Leo turned to go but Mabel's voice stopped her.

"What's the matter with you? You ain't going to give Mabel a hug or nothing?"

Leo leaned over and felt Mabel's powerful arms engulf her. "I'm sorry, Mabel. I didn't mean to be bad."

"You ain't bad, child; you're just too young to understand some things." Mabel turned away, pretending to have something in her eye. "Just promise Mabel you'll be good for your Momma. Promise me you won't talk bad about that school while you're home."

In Mabel's arms Leo felt protected, safe, like she was five-years-old again. "I promise, Mabel."

Mabel let go of her and smiled. "Good. Now get your things unpacked and let me get my floor finished."

Leo went to her room and, after running her hand across the made bed, laid down on it. It felt good to be in her own bed, her own room. She looked up at the picture of the Sacred Heart Of Jesus. Like Mabel's arms, it made her feel little. Jesus loved little children, except, perhaps, ones who made their mothers feel bad, made them cry. She hadn't meant to. She loved her mother more than anyone else. She pulled the leather visor from her pocket. Mabel was right: she was selfish. Her mother had enough to worry about.

She laid the visor on her pillow and rested her head beside it. The leather still smelled of smoke. "I won't make Ma feel bad again," Leo promised the Jesus hanging on the wall. "And I won't tell her nothing about school, even if she asks."

Leo woke up an hour later. The upstairs was dark, and when she entered the bright kitchen, the lights stung her eyes. Maggie was setting the table, her mother was at the stove, mashing potatoes, Mikey and Hal were playing checkers.

"Where's Mark?" she asked, rubbing her eyes.

"He's got a job at the new discount store," Hal said. "Walks five miles each way, just so he doesn't have to spend a nickel on the bus."

Leo smiled. Mark was the only one who took

his bank account seriously and saved every penny he got.

"Will he be home for supper?"

Hal moved a red checker. "Never is anymore."

"Hal's g-got a job, t-too," Mikey said proudly.

Hal changed jobs as fast as he changed girlfriends, about every two weeks. He'd done everything from paper routes to selling popcorn at the Shrine circus.

"Where now?" asked Leo.

"The car wash," said Hal, smiling. "I live for Saturdays. Do you have any idea how many beautiful women need their cars washed?"

Sliding his checker into place, Mikey said, "K-king me."

Hal looked surprised. "Where'd he come from you little snot?"

Mikey beamed. "Y-you're g-good at g-girlfriends b-but n-not checkers."

Leo sat on the stool absorbing it all, Maggie putting out the plates, her mother making supper, Hal and Mikey's game in progress. The room was warm with everything she'd missed.

She watched her mother turn the fish in the cast iron pan. By the way her mother was moving, Leo could tell her back was hurting again. When her mother was in nursing school, she'd slipped on some icy stairs and broke her back. She'd had to stay in a full body cast for months, and her back still bothered her. Now she had to sleep with a board under her mattress, and on a bad day, she couldn't even get out of bed.

Once the meal was prepared, their mother served them, not bothering to eat herself. She hovered over them making sure everything was hot, plentiful, and perfect.

"Ma, this fish is excellent," Hal told her. "Why don't you have some?"

"I'll eat later."

"Sure beats school food," said Leo, then remembering her promise, added, "Not that the food there isn't good, it's just no one makes fish like you can."

"Well, you eat all you want. I made it special for you girls."

"Thanks, Ma," said Maggie. "And we'll clean things up here, so don't worry about the dishes."

"I knew there was a reason I missed you," said Hal.

"If everyone's all set, I'm going upstairs," said their mother. "I need to lie down for awhile."

"We're in good shape, Ma," Hal assured her. "Give your back a rest."

"Can I get you anything else before I go, Leo?"

Leo looked up at her mother who looked tired and pale. "No thanks, Ma. This is great."

"All right then, I'll be in my room."

After their mother had left the kitchen, Leo asked Hal, "So where's the Old Man?"

"Who cares," said Hal, then laughed as though he didn't mean it.

At the mention of their father, Leo noticed Mikey looked toward the door.

"I-I'm all done." Mikey pushed his plate away,

then collected his checkers and left the room.

Leo watched him go, then looked quizzically at Hal.

Hal's face lost it's permanent smile. "It's the Old Man," he said, looking away.

"What about him?" asked Maggie.

Hal was silent for a moment, frowning with indecision. "Ma said you guys didn't need to know about it."

"Tell us," said Leo, "Maggie will forget about it tomorrow, anyhow."

"As if," Maggie told her, then turned to Hal. "Tell us."

When Hal finally spoke his voice had a hard edge to it. "Last weekend he took off down the street in his bathrobe and slippers. The bastard told Mikey he was going to lie down in the middle of Brighton Avenue and wait till a truck ran him over. Scared the crap out of Mikey. He chased after him, bawling his eyes out. Mikey really believed the Old Man was going to do it."

Leo and Maggie sat still and Hal continued.

"He's half in the bag all the time now. He might even loose his job. It's killing Ma."

"So what happened? With Mikey, I mean," asked Leo.

"Ma sent me after them. The Old Man never got past Mrs. Hayes'. He didn't remember a thing after I sobered him up. Puked his guts out, then had a reaction that night."

"Poor Mikey," said Maggie. "No wonder his stuttering's worse."

"Mikey won't go near him now," Hal told them. "Won't even try to play checkers with him."

"What else happened while we were gone?" asked Maggie.

"A lot of stuff, even worse than that. But you don't need to hear it . . . There is something else, but Ma wanted to tell you about it herself."

"What is it?" Maggie persisted.

"I can't," Hal said in a tone of finality. "I promised her I wouldn't say anything." Then he laughed and made goo-goo eyes at them. "So any beautiful rich girls at your school dying to go out with me? You showed them a picture of me, didn't you?"

"Hope." Maggie looked at Leo and they both laughed.

"If you're laughing like that," said Hal, "she must be muggly."

They sat at the counter, Leo pushing the remnants of her meal around her plate as Hal entertained them with funny stories about school. He also told them how he'd gotten arrested at a dance at the Expo for inciting a riot when all he was doing was dancing. They'd taken him to the station and when the cop called home, their father had told him, "Keep him there till morning." Hal made it all sound like a joke, but Leo could tell he was still angry about it.

"Mark and him have gotten into it a few times, too," Hal continued. "I don't blame him; the Old Man's always on his back. Mark's problem is he doesn't know how to handle him, especially when he's out of it. He went and told the Old Man he was nothing but a drunk destroying his family. I don't have to tell you the fists flew over that one."

They heard the side door open, the sound of his step in the hall.

"Speak of the devil," Hal said under his breath.

Maggie and Leo got up and started clearing the table. Leo heard her father come into the kitchen but didn't turn around.

"Hi, Dad," said Hal brightly. "Leo and Maggie have been dying to see you. They just asked when you'd be home."

"Don't believe him," said Maggie, as she left the room.

Leo watched Maggie go, wanting to follow her.

Her father laid his keys and pipe down on the table. "What about you?" he asked her. "You glad to see me, too?"

Leo's mouth felt thick, she swallowed hard. I . . . I missed you."

"You don't have to lie, Leo."

"I'm not lying."

"Take a ride with me, then. I want to talk to you about something."

Leo looked toward Hal for help.

"Can I come, too, Dad?" asked her brother.

"No, just your sister. You already know about it."

"I've got to get my coat." Leo brushed by him, smelling the alcohol.

When she passed the back stairs she heard a voice whisper from the darkness, "Don't go Leo."

Leo looked at her sister. "I'll be all right," she told her.

"Tell him you don't want to go," Maggie urged.

"I already said I would."

As they drove to the Western Prom, Leo tried to remember the last time she'd ridden alone with her father and couldn't. When she was little, and he didn't drink all the time, he used to take her everywhere. He knew a man at the fire station near Patches who would let her crawl all over the fire trucks. And, sometimes, he'd take her down to Nino's because he knew the man who owned the store, and she'd get free animal crackers. But she'd always liked the Western Prom the best, especially at night. Up there she could see all the lights in Libbytown, and the airport, and the big clock at Union Station that had a face like the moon. Her father had taken her up to the Prom the day they'd torn down Union Station. She'd watched the big crane, its ball swinging into the bricks, the dust blowing like smoke. There had been a lot of people watching, one man was even crying. Her father had told her not to stare at him. In place of the magical train station, they'd put up a shopping center--a long rectangular building that looked like something Mikey could make.

Now he rarely took her anywhere, and when he did, he usually ended up embarrassing her. Since the last father daughter banquet they'd gone to for the Knights of Columbus, Maggie wouldn't even get in the car with him unless she had to. At the banquet, he'd had a diabetic reaction. She and Maggie were off playing games so they didn't notice it was coming. By the time they got back to their table to eat, he was well on his way. The other fathers were all around him saying he was drunk, but she and Maggie knew better, they could always tell the difference. She tried to tell them what was happening, but they wouldn't listen; they didn't even know what a reaction was. Maggie finally went and got the juice and sugar herself from the cook in the kitchen. Then, while Maggie held his head back, Leo forced him to drink it. Everyone watched them. Everyone saw the juice run down his chin. They all looked at him as though he was some kind of freak, and she wanted to tell them to go to hell because they were so stupid. When he finally came out of it, he apologized to anyone who would listen. Then they left. This year, he didn't ask her or Maggie to go.

When they got to the Prom, her father stopped the car and shut off the lights. Leo edged toward the door letting the darkness separate them.

Her father cleared his throat, then took a puff off his pipe. "I'm going away for awhile."

Hearing him say that triggered a clear memory. When they were little, they would pile on his bed every night to hear him tell stories. The lights would be out and the window always open because he liked his room cold. Their favorite story was how he was going to fix up an old school bus and take them to Alaska to hunt for gold.

"Are you going to Alaska?" she asked him now.

"No," he replied. "To Boston--to a hospital. I'm going to get some help. . . It'll be best all the way around. I've fouled things up here. Everyone hates me now. You kids, your mother. . ."

Why shouldn't they hate him, she asked herself, trying to picture Mikey running down the street after him. Mikey, who cried when a bug got squished, who loved him more than any of them, believed him when he'd said he was going to lie down in the middle of the road. And what about Mark, who kept the yard looking better than a golf course, who got straight A's, who, no matter how hard he tried to please him, never could. And Hal, who always sobered him up, how did he feel sitting in jail all night knowing he wouldn't come and get him? And what about their mother, who only cried when she thought no one was listening, who didn't want to send them away, but had to, because of him.

Why shouldn't they hate him? Why shouldn't she?

"I don't hate you," she said, surprised that the words had come out of her mouth, and that she meant them.

"I wouldn't blame you if you did. If it weren't for me, you wouldn't be in that damn school. Your mother told me about your hat when I talked to her on the phone."

"When do you have to go?" she asked.

"Tomorrow. I wanted to tell you myself. I

103

figured your sister wouldn't care one way or the other, and I didn't tell Mikey, either. It would be better if your mother tells him after I'm gone."

"How long do you have to stay there?"

"I don't know. As long as it takes."

She looked out at the red and blue dots twinkling at the airport. From where they were parked, she could almost make out Thompson's Point just beyond Hobo Jungle. "Can I write to you?"

"If you want to."

She moved away from the door, just a little closer to him.

The next morning, Leo sat on the front steps beside her father's big leather suitcase. Hal and Mark had already gone to work, Mikey was off playing, and Maggie was hiding so she wouldn't have to say good-bye. Leo had thought that with her father going away, maybe she and Maggie would be able to stay home. But Maggie had put that hope to rest. "Ma don't know if he's gonna stay there until he's better. Besides, they've already paid for us to go to school, stupid."

When the taxi drove up, her father came out wearing a suit. For a moment he stood on the porch looking at her mother in the doorway. Then he picked up his bag.

Leo jumped off the steps. "You want me to

carry that, Dad?"

"No, Leo. I've got it," he said, moving down the walk.

Leo tagged behind, watched the taxi driver get out and open the trunk, put the bag in.

Her father hesitated for a moment before climbing into the back seat. "You be good for your mother," he said, then clumsily patted Leo's shoulder.

By that awkward pat, that still felt hot were it landed, she knew her father was trying to say, "I love you."

"Don't give her any trouble."

"I won't," she whispered.

Watching the yellow car inch away from the curb, she felt a rush of love and sadness. She stared at the back of her father's head, waiting for him to turn in his seat and wave. There were so many things she'd wanted to say: I love you; I don't blame you; I want you to love me, too. But it was too late.

VII.

LESSONS IN
LIFE AND DEATH

Back at school, Leo continued to carry her visor everywhere. She kept it in the pocket of her uniform, its bulging presence displayed like a badge of courage. She almost believed it had magical powers that could ward off Sister St. Paul, for most of the time, the nun stayed away from her. Although Sister St. Paul still got after her about running in the hall, pulling up her socks, and polishing her shoes, she'd never once asked Leo what she had stuffed in her pocket.

At St. Christopher's, Leo's school work improved greatly. With five hours of study hall to sit through six days a week at the Academy, she had to do something. She memorized all the states and capitols in America, all the countries in Europe, and read three to four books a week. Occasionally, there would be a break in the mundane routine. Every other Friday night there was no evening study hall, and the girls were allowed to spend the two-and-a-half hours listening to records and dancing in the rec hall. Hands down, Evette was the best dancer, and often picked Leo for her partner, teaching her how to do the Jerk and the Slide. And on Halloween they'd had a costume party. Calsa, who Maggie called The Queen Of Demerits, went as a nun. Evette went as Harriet Tubman, and Maggie a cheerleader. Having no costume to wear, Leo tied a large brown sponge on her head, painted a big black "2" on her face, and went as a pencil.

As the weeks slipped by, the maple trees that lined the school's driveway turned crimson, the nights turned colder, and, on the fourth of November, Leo turned eleven. Sister Alphonse's birthday gift was a holy card, Angie's a candy bar, Maggie's eleven whacks with a pinch to grow on.

It had been a lonely birthday despite her mother's phone call and package from home. All week she'd waited for a card from her father. The year before he'd given her a blue bike for her birthday; this year, he'd forgotten all about her. She told Maggie it didn't matter, all that mattered was that he was at that hospital trying to get better, trying to "dry out" as Hal put it. Maggie's response was, "Don't get your hopes up."

Leo knew what her sister meant--he was always making promises he would never keep: all the swim meets he said he would come to; all the outings they never got to; all the times he told Mikey, "maybe later." Like Maggie, she worried that this promise would be broken, too. She was almost afraid to believe he would really stop drinking. But she wanted him to, and every night before she went to bed, she prayed to Jesus that he would.

A week after her birthday, as she and Angie sat in the woods with the last of the leaves falling down around them; they continued their conversation from recess.

"Hey, it's the truth, no kidding," Angie told her. "They were parked on the dirt road next to Benson's field."

"And they didn't have no clothes on?"

"Nope, not a thing."

"What were they doing?'

"I don't know. Something bad. I ran like hell."

"Debbie Victor on my swim team says people make babies when they take their clothes off," Leo told her. "But it's got to be a man and a woman and they've got to be married . . . Think they were making a baby?"

"Must of been." Angie's eyes grew bigger as she looked at Leo. "My mother and father must of got naked three times. I'm never gettin' married; no kidding. No boy's ever gonna see me without my clothes on."

"Debbie said when you get older you're supposed to like gettin' naked. Sorta like your supposed to like peas when you grow up."

"I bet Olive will love gettin' naked," laughed Angie. "She wears those see-through blouses all the time now, just so everyone knows she wears a bra."

"Hal calls them over-the-shoulder-boulder-holders," said Leo, and both girls giggled.

"I don't ever want to wear one," Leo continued.

"As soon as you do, you start getting queer about boys. It happened to Maggie. Now that's all she thinks about. You should hear her on the phone."

"Old Olive's queer about boys, all right," said Angie. "Rosa said she went to first base with Timmy Barnes."

"First base?" questioned Leo.

"You know, kissed him on the lips."

"I caught Maggie practicing on her hand once. She said she'd kill me if I ever told anyone . . . Were those people in the car kissing?"

"I only saw them for a second, but they looked like they were wrestling. I got out of there fast. Didn't stop running till I got to the junk store."

"Did you tell your mother?"

"You kidding?"

"When I told Jack how Debbie said babies were made, he said I should talk to my mother. But I asked Maggie instead."

"What'd she say?"

"She said when I got her age, Ma would give me a book to read."

All the way back to the Academy, Leo thought about Angie's secret. She couldn't imagine why anyone would want to make a baby in a car, or why they had to be naked to get one. The thought of ever wanting to kiss a boy on the lips was bad enough. But, she told herself, if she ever did have to have a boyfriend when she got old, she'd want it to be Jack.

When she was home on free-weekend, she'd dropped by Jack's house, but he wasn't there. His mother, who always wore lipstick and the kind of clothes other mothers only wore to church, had asked her in for cookies and lemonade. While she ate the snack, Jack's mother told her he'd given up the paper route. Now that he was in high school and playing football on the freshman team, he didn't have time for it. Leo was worried that if he didn't have time for the paper route anymore, then maybe he wouldn't have time for her, either. The hell with him, she thought; he hasn't even sent me a letter.

A week before they were to go home for Thanksgiving, Leo woke up to sunlight coming through the dorm windows. "What's going on?" she asked. "Is it Saturday?"

Some of the other girls were sitting up in bed, looking just as puzzled. Saturday was the only day they were allowed to sleep until seven, the only day of the week they didn't get up in the dark. But this was Tuesday.

"Maybe the bell's broken," said Calsa.

Then Sister Theresa came into the dorm and cleared up the mystery. "I'm afraid I have some sad news, girls," she told them. "Father Richie's mother died during the night."

Poor Fish Eyes, thought Leo.

"Of course this means Chapel and all classes have been canceled for the day."

"You mean there's no school?" asked Leo. "At St. Christopher's, too?"

"Yes, Leona, there will be no school at St. Christopher's as well."

"All right!" exclaimed Leo, and some of the girls giggled.

"Leona!"

"Oh, sorry, Sister. I didn't mean it that way. I was just so glad about not having school I forgot about Father Richie."

"You wouldn't have forgotten if it were your mother," said the nun, and the point was not lost on Leo or any of the others.

After breakfast and chores, the girls spent two hours of silence in the chapel. They were supposed to be praying for Father Richie's mother, helping her soul make its way to heaven. Leo figured his mother's soul was already there--her son was a priest; God wouldn't make her wait in line. So after one quick Hail Mary and an Our Father, she used the rest of the time as if it were study hall. Carefully holding her missal so no one could see the copy of *Lord Of The Flies* tucked inside, she left the chapel and silent praying behind to join Piggy, Ralph, and the other boys on the island with no grownups.

That afternoon, Sister St. Paul told them they were going to pay their respects to Father Richie at Herbert's Funeral Parlor. Leo didn't have a clue what Sister meant, but she was happy to be going somewhere.

It felt great to be off the campus and away from those brick walls, great to be outside in the sunshine when she would have been in school. She skipped along as the blue line of girls marched across town like soldiers, the nuns in the front and rear, keeping order like generals: "No talking." "Keep in line, girls." "Stop skipping, Leona."

Leo still didn't have a clue about the mission, until they entered the funeral parlor. To the right, as she came in, there was a double doorway, and through its entrance she could see into a room, could see the handful of mingling grownups, and the stands of flowers bordering each side of the casket.

"There's a dead person in there," she whispered to Maggie. "I can see his head."

Sister Theresa tapped Leo on the shoulder, and placing her finger to her lips, told her, "Shhh."

Leo turned back around, then followed the girls in front of her as they filed by two's into a large room. The room was softly lit and smelled of flowers. Through the gaps in the line, she watched the girls kneel in pairs before a casket. As her turn drew closer, she began to tremble. I don't want to go up there, she thought. I don't want pray in front of a dead body. She glanced behind her, looking for a place to run, but a wall of nuns blocked the only exit. She looked up at Doris, who was her partner, and as though sensing Leo's fear, the older girl took her hand. The two of them went together, and Doris let go of Leo's hand so they could bless themselves as they knelt.

Leo could barely see over the casket; her face was eye level with Father Richie's mother. She was too afraid to pray. She stared at the folded hands, at the blue rosary beads wound around the white fingers. Although she didn't want to look, her eyes traveled up the white silk blouse with its high collar and gold cross, to the still face, wrinkled and powdered; took in the woman's wire-rim glasses resting in place above her closed lids; and her hair, the color of snow. Suddenly she had the urge to touch her, to make sure she was real or dead, and when her curious fingers touched the woman's shoulder the stiffness took her by surprise.

Seeing Leo reach out and touch the body took Doris by surprise. She jumped up from the kneeler and her quick movement made Leo jump, too.

"Over here girls," Sister Theresa whispered to them. "Once you've paid your respects to Father Richie, you can line up outside with the others.

Father Richie was standing beside Sister St. Paul, receiving condolences and shaking hands with each girl as they left. When it was Leo's turn, she told him, "I haven't learned the prayer for giving respects yet. But I'm sorry for you, Father. I know how I felt when my dog died."

Sister St. Paul locked onto Leo's shoulder with her fingers. "Move right along now, Leona, the others are waiting."

Father Richie brushed Sister St. Paul's hand aside. "One moment, Sister." The priest bent down and took both of Leo's hands in his. "Thank you, Leona. What you said was very kind. And I want you to know, there's no right or wrong way to tell someone you're sorry if it comes from the heart."

"That's how I figure it, too, Father."

The priest smiled at her, then turned to Sister St. Paul. "We can learn great things from God's children. Don't you agree, Sister?"

"Absolutely, Father."

Outside on the sidewalk, Leo watched the cars drive by while she and the other girls waited. She could hear the whispers through the line: "Did you see her hands?" "Did you see...did you see...did you see..." Leo didn't want to listen. She concentrated on the cars, wishing one of them would stop and offer her a ride. She'd go anywhere they'd take her. Anywhere but back inside. The whole thing didn't seem right to her. Having your mother laid out in a box for strangers to stare at, to pray over. If she'd been Father Richie, she would have told them all to get the hell out.

She was angry for him, angry for herself. They should have warned her; they should have told her-- they shouldn't have let her walk inside that house with its sweet smelling flowers without knowing.

It was the first dead person she'd ever seen.

She didn't even know her name, this woman, who still wore her glasses, whose body was as hard as the ground. And as she stood on the sidewalk, feeling cold as ice, the fear, anger, and sadness made her hate those nuns even more.

VIII.

THANKSGIVING

L eo tagged behind Hal at a safe distance, the
memory of last year's game fresh in her mind.
Every Thanksgiving the Deering Rams played the
Portland High Bulldogs in football. The rival
schools had been playing this traditional game long
before her father graduated from Deering in the mid-
thirties, and every year since she was little, he'd
taken her to the game.

She stopped a few steps behind Hal, watching
him adjust his tweed cap in the window of a parked
car. Her brother hadn't said one word during the
two-mile walk to the stadium. He was still mad
about having to take her. He'd been elected because
her father was still in the hospital, and her mother
wouldn't let her go alone.

As they stood in line at the stadium, Hal
pretended she wasn't with him. Those under twelve
got in free and, while Hal was buying his ticket, she
walked through the gate by herself. To hell with

him, she thought, and struck off on her own to find a good seat.

She wormed her way through the crowd, the air smelling of popcorn and burgers, and got a center seat in the bleachers. Sitting on Portland's side seemed strange, but Hal and Jack went to Portland and she thought it best to sit there. Besides, Jack's mother said he was playing on the Freshman team; maybe she'd get to see him in his uniform. Looking across the field at the purple signs waving in the Deering stands, she felt a little guilty. Her father had been the water boy for the Deering Rams when he was in high school--the next time she wrote to him, she'd tell him she sat on Deering's side so he wouldn't feel bad.

On fall Sundays, football was the only program they ever watched at her house. No one even dared to change the channel during commercials, unless there was a game on another station. Her father used to say, "Like it or lump it, this is what we're watching." She'd learned to like it. Her father had taught her the rules, the plays, the names of the teams. By half-time she'd come to the conclusion that watching the Thanksgiving game without him wasn't much fun. Especially since she was sitting on Portland's side while rooting for Deering. Once, when she stood and cheered for a Deering field goal, she thought the man next to her was going to hit her.

While the players retreated to the locker rooms, she fought through the crowd to the concession stand. Jingling the change in her pocket, she contemplated biting into one of the stadium's famous hot dogs, but when she rounded the corner, she stopped abruptly.

"Hey, Leo!" called Jack, who was leaning against the fence.

She'd already spotted him, and the blonde girl who was hanging all over his coat. "Oh, hi Jack," she said, walking over to them. "How come you're not playing? Ain't you good enough?"

"Still a wise guy." Jack reached out and tussled her hair. "Hey, where's your hat?"

Leo avoided the question with a shrug.

Jack slipped his arm around the blonde and asked another. "So how's that boarding school?"

"They haven't kicked me out yet, if that's what you mean."

"Who's this?" asked the girl. "One of your cousins?"

Leo gave her a disgusted look. "I'd rather be dead than related to him."

Jack laughed. "She's Hal's little sister. Can't you tell?"

The girl looked at Leo with more interest. "I'm Nancy Traits. Nice to meet you."

"So you're Nancy Traits. Wow, Hal talks about you all the time. He thinks you're beautiful."

Nancy blushed and said sweetly, "No, he doesn't."

"He sure does. All the time. I bet he'd ask you out if he wasn't so scared you'd stiff him."

"You do? Oh, you're just kidding." Nancy moved away from Jack.

"I'm sure of it," Leo lied. "No kidding." She

looked at Jack and smiled. "Do you see much of Bertha anymore?"

"Who's Bertha?" asked Nancy.

"Oh, she was Jack's girlfriend down at the pool," said Leo, trying not to laugh.

Jack shot her a get lost look, and Leo took him up on it. "See you later, Jack. Maybe next year they'll let you play." She easily dodged his fake punch, then called over her shoulder, "Hope Deering wins!"

Leo walked through the gate then headed down Park Ave. Jack, what a jerk, putting his arm around that girl just to show off. She turned, looking toward the stadium, the sound of the crowd carrying in the wind--boy, Old Hal was going to get it.

She cut down Douglas Street, deciding to take a quick walk by the pool before going home. Strolling up to the fence, she stared through the network of metal diamonds at the empty pool. It seems so different, she thought, just like home. Without her father around, things were better. It wasn't something she could put into words, it was a feeling. Everyone acted happier, laughed more. Mikey was hardly stuttering and their mother didn't stay in her room half as much. Maggie even had some of her friends over and no one in the family ever did that. It was like that tight feeling she'd felt in the house all summer had found a different house to live in.

Standing there, her fingers curled around cold metal, her eyes focused on the empty pool, the gray sky and the quiet rekindled the scary dream. She'd had it almost every night since paying her respects, and always it was the same. She was in a small room with a big black crow that had hands instead of claws. The bird was bigger than she was and it was pulling her toward the box she collected trash in. She didn't want to look inside the box, but the crow had her by the back of the neck and made her, made her look down at her mother who was laid out as though she were dead. She'd never told anyone about the dream, not even Angie. She was afraid if she did, it might come true.

Letting go of the fence, she hurried toward home, shivering from the vivid memory and its power to frighten her even in daylight.

"Ma's rippin'; you're going to get it. You might as well eat down at the Sportsmen's Grill," Maggie told Hal when he walked in.

"Is Leo home?"

"What's it to you? Taking off on her."

"She took off on me!"

"That's not what she told Ma."

"That little brat. Wait till I get my hands on her."

Leo raced into the kitchen. She'd overheard the conversation and knew she'd better keep out of Hal's way. "Ma, do you want me to bring anything else out?" she asked sweetly.

"Take the rolls on the counter, but don't eat any."

"I won't." Leo grabbed the basket of rolls, and hustled into the dining room. Crossing the gold carpet, she noticed the arrangement of dried flowers Mark had put inside the fireplace for decoration. It looked nice. Mark had a way of making things look good; he knew what lights to turn on; where to put vases and things.

After placing the basket on the table, she picked up one of the silver knives and coated a warm roll with butter. Stuffing half of it in her mouth, she tiptoed back into the pantry to hear Hal get it.

"I asked you to do one simple thing. Take your sister to the game."

"I told you, she took off on me. I was getting my ticket and when I turned around, she was gone. What do you want? I spent the whole friggin' game looking for her."

"Watch your language," their mother said curtly.

"I even had them page her at the half."

"Well, she wouldn't have heard it. She was almost home by then."

Popping the rest of the roll into her mouth, Leo leaned closer to the door, peeking through the crack. Her mother was working on the turkey. Hal was standing next to her, still in his coat and cap.

"She said you wouldn't even talk to her. Wouldn't even walk with her. Your own sister."

"Listen, Ma, the little brat took off on me and that's that."

"No, you listen. With your father gone, I need help. I thought I could depend on you. I should have had Mark take her."

"Maybe you should have. He's your favorite anyway."

Hal stormed out of the room and Leo heard him say, "I'm going to kill her." She put her hand over her mouth to stifle a laugh and retreated to the dining room.

Mikey was standing there gazing at the table.

"What'cha doing?" she asked.

"Just looking," he said. "It's n-nice. I like the turkey candles."

"Me, too. Where are you going to sit?"

"Right here." Mikey climbed up on the chair, then told her, "I like Thanksgiving b-because you don't have to go to church."

Maggie carried in a tray full of serving dishes, each steaming with a different kind of vegetable. Leo got up and helped her place them around the table.

"Thanks," said Maggie. "I just got one more load to go."

Hal swaggered in, took a seat by the rolls, and proceeded to glare at Leo. Maggie returned with the cranberry sauce and boiled onions, and after setting them down, she set herself down in a chair beside Mikey.

Leo finally returned Hal's glare with a sheepish look. "Did Portland loose?"

"Don't even talk to me," he said.

"Cut it out you guys," snapped Maggie. "Ma's been up since four o'clock this morning making this meal. You wreck it and I'll beat the crap out of both of you."

After glancing around the room and looking under the table, Hal said, "For a minute there, I thought I heard the Old Man."

They all laughed at the comparison, except for Mikey, who didn't get it, then they watched Mark come through the pantry door with a serving dish of mashed potatoes in his hands. Their mother was right behind him, carrying the turkey on a platter. She laid it on the table, then let out an exhausted sigh.

Leo looked at her mother; there were pin pricks of sweat on her forehead. "Sit down, Ma," she told her.

"I can't, I have to get the gravy."

"I'll get it." Maggie jumped up and headed for the kitchen.

While they waited for Maggie, Leo's gaze was drawn to the empty chair at the head of the table. Everyone had made a big deal about where they were going to sit, and she figured it was because no one wanted to sit there: it was their father's place.

Maggie returned with the gravy and, once she was seated, they all bowed their heads.

"Bless us Our Lord . . ."

Leo lifted her eyes slightly, watching her mother's sad face as she said grace. She misses him, too, she thought.

" . . . for these gifts we are about to receive, through Christ Our Lord, Amen."

For a moment no one moved, all eyes looking toward the empty chair, all unsure how to begin the feast without his presence.

Finally, Hal stood and reached for the carving knife, but Mark's hand got to it first. "I'm the oldest," said Mark. "I'll carve."

Leo looked from brother to brother. Hal was wearing jeans and a red flannel shirt: Mark, a jacket and tie. They sure are different, she thought. Mark wore cuff links and Hal didn't even own a shirt that needed them.

Hal retreated to his chair. "Just make sure you give me a drumstick."

For awhile, everyone kept their thoughts to themselves, the clatter of dishes helping to fill the void of silence. Leo took small helpings of each item even though she didn't like most of the vegetables. She figured if her mother worked so hard to prepare them, she could at least put them on her plate.

"Stop daydreaming, Leona, and eat something."

Leo looked at her mother, then at her plate--she wasn't hungry. She noticed no one except Mikey was eating much, either.

"Great bird, Ma!" said Hal, waving his drumstick.

Mark wiped the corners of his mouth with his napkin. "The stuffing's delicious."

Leo had the feeling that if she looked up she would see her father sitting there. It was the same feeling she'd had after her dog died. For days she'd kept expecting to see or hear him around the house, then she'd remember. "I wonder if Dad's having a turkey dinner," she said, looking toward his chair.

The forks seemed to stop in midair.

"Hey, guess who I saw at the game?" said Hal.

"Who?" Mikey asked in a small voice.

"Steve Garney."

Everyone laughed.

"You should have asked him to come over and clean the garage." Mark smiled, his braces flashing.

"Remember that?" Hal continued. "Steve was out in the garage waiting for me, and Dad didn't have his glasses on and thought Steve was me and told him to clean it up. I went out, and there's Steve cleaning the garage and Dad's sitting on the steps watching him to make sure he did a good job."

"Hasn't been as clean since," laughed Maggie.

Their mother shook her head slowly. "He can't see if he doesn't wear his glasses."

"How about the time he was in the hospital and they wouldn't let him come home for his anniversary," said Mark, pushing aside his plate. "Remember that, Ma?"

"How could I forget?" she said, smiling. "He tied sheets together and climbed out the second story window. Took a cab across town in his bathrobe and slippers in the dead of winter."

"Why wouldn't they let him come home, Ma?" asked Leo. It was the first time she'd heard this one.

"He'd just had his eyes operated on and had gotten an infection."

"Didn't anyone see him escaping?" questioned Leo.

"It was in the middle of the night," said Mark.

"When I opened that door and saw him standing

there in his bathrobe . . . in February, mind you! I just about died." Their mother's eyes grew misty, and for a moment everyone was silent.

"Can we call him?" Mark asked softly.

Their mother looked around the table. "When we're finished."

"C-can I talk?" asked Mikey.

"Just for a minute. My bills this month are sky high."

"That's okay, Ma," Mikey told her. "A minute's a long t-time."

IX.

SILENT NIGHT

In the schoolyard, Leo leaned against the steel monkey bars, thinking about the poor can. Since Thanksgiving, her class had taken up a collection in a tin can wrapped with Christmas paper. Every day, pennies, nickels, and dimes went through the slot in the plastic cover. Sister Marie had told them it would buy a present for a needy family.

Leo cocked her head at Angie. "Did you see how hot Olive Oil thought she was when she put that dollar in the poor can?"

"She was the same way when we collected for the pagan babies," Angie responded. "Acts like she died and became a saint. She thinks she's a millionaire just because her father owns a crummy pharmacy."

Leo pulled her mittens over her chapped hands. "Who'd name their kid Olive, anyhow? It's like calling your kid pickle. No wonder she's so weird."

Angie hung on the monkey bar like a coat on a clothesline. "She'd be weird even if her name was Mary. Wearing nylons to school when it's gonna snow."

"Joe said we're supposed to get four inches."

"I don't know why you bother to listen to him," said Angie, dismounting gracefully from the bar. "He's stayed back twice already. If he passes this year, he'll be lucky."

"I don't think he's as dumb as everybody thinks," said Leo, looking toward the Academy. "He just don't like school." She turned and watched Angie collect her books. "Did I tell you my father's coming home for Christmas?"

"They're letting him out for three days, you got his letter yesterday, and you've only told me about ten times." Angie grinned at her. "But that's okay."

"Hey!" Doris stood by the window in the rec hall, pointing. "Look!"

"What is it?" someone asked.

"It's snowing!" she announced.

"Whoopee," Hope said, sarcastically. "Maybe we can build a snowman."

Leo ran over to the windows, and fought for a view among the other girls. Peering out, her nose squished against the glass, she saw a thin layer of white sticking to the frozen ground. Old Joe was right, she thought.

A second later the Mexicans were running around the courtyard.

Hope shook her head. "Look at them."

Leo stared up at Hope instead, taking in the close cropped hair. It makes her look like a boy, she thought. A few weeks back, she'd walked into the bathroom and there was Hope, hacking off her long blonde hair with a pair of scissors. "They don't get snow in Mexico," Leo told her.

"No kidding." Hope tapped her fingers on the window. "Christ, they're trying to eat it," she said in disgust.

Leo left her and ran outside to join the others. The frigid night air bit through her uniform as she watched the dark skinned girls, who usually complained about the cold, play coatless in the snow. Despite their laughing voices, it was oddly quiet, and that familiar silence linked with falling snow came back to her unexpectedly.

Sister Theresa opened the door and, standing sideways, called the girls in. Leo looked up at the nun's dark figure silhouetted against the lighted doorway. For a heartbeat, she looked just like her father--the sideways stance, the arm holding back the door. It was the ritual of not making eight o'clock curfew--"Get in here.". . ."No you're going to hit me.". . . "I'm not going to hit you, get in here.". . ."You promise you won't hit me?". . . "I said get in here." Nine out of ten times, she'd get a clout on the way in.

"Hurry up, Leo," called Sister Theresa. "It's freezing, you'll catch your death."

Leo walked slowly to the bottom of the steps, then looked up at the nun. "Are you going to hit me?"

The Christmas spirit infiltrated the school. Classroom walls wore cardboard angels and reindeer; blackboards captured Christmas scenes in colored chalk. In the chapel, a hand-carved nativity was set up, its empty manger waiting for baby Jesus. Even the halls were decorated, taking on the scent of evergreen from wreaths with red velvet bows.

Leo stood in front of the tree in the rec hall. Behind her, excited voices chattered about the evening's Christmas party, or where they were going for the holidays, or what they were getting for Christmas; while the sad-eyed Mexicans huddled in a clump in the corner, wistfully remembering home. In the distance, like the volume of a T.V. turned down low, came the voices of the seniors practicing *Silent Night* for the umpteenth time.

Leo reached out and touched one of the more intricate ornaments, a tiny winter scene painted inside an egg shell. Every student had made an ornament for the tree. She'd made a small star out of tinfoil, and noticed that someone had placed it on the side facing the wall where no one could see it.

Beneath the tree were presents. They'd exchanged names by picking them out of a large jar. She'd gotten Marisa's name, but had no idea what she was giving her. Her mother had sent the gift in the mail, already wrapped. Maggie thought it was jewelry because of the box. Maggie was an expert on figuring out presents. If she couldn't guess what it was by shaking and feeling, she'd hold it up to the light and see if she could read the box through the wrapping. If that didn't work, she'd make a tiny tear in the paper, right beneath the bow. Maggie always knew what a gift was before she opened it. Leo didn't want to know; she liked surprises.

Withdrawing her hand from the ornament, her mind wandered back to Joe. After school, she'd forgotten her father's Christmas card, and had run back to her classroom to get it. She was surprised to see Joe and Sister Marie still there. Joe was holding a present, a box shaped like those that clothes came in. He'd quickly shoved it into a grocery bag, his face turning the shade of the present's red bow. Watching him, she'd realized all their pennies, nickels, and Olive's dollar collected in the poor can, had been used to buy Joe that present. Joe wouldn't look at her. He mumbled "Merry Christmas" to Sister Marie, then hurried out of the classroom.

After retrieving the card, she ran out of the room and caught up with him just as he was going out of the building. She got close enough to touch him, then whispered, "I won't tell, Joe."

He ignored her, pushed the door open, and left her standing there. She watched him run down the steps, then move across the snow, holding onto his bag like it was garbage.

Leo touched a strand of tinsel, her finger

tapping it into motion, then she walked around the back of the tree where her tinfoil star was hiding. She moved the star to a branch in front, right beside the egg ornament.

"Too bad we don't have food like this all the time." Leo took another mouthful of roast beef. "I think they just give us decent meals before holidays so we'll go home and tell our parents how good the food is."

Calsa's cackle shot across the table, almost blowing out the candle. Leo looked at her and smiled, then glanced around the cafeteria. It looked nice by candlelight. All the tables had white cloths on them, candles, and little red baskets of nuts and mints. The girls were dressed up for the occasion, many of them wearing long dresses. She noticed that everyone was speaking softly, unlike the usual roar. They should eat by candlelight all the time, she thought.

"You think Hope could have worn something besides her uniform," said Maggie.

"Her parents are taking her to the Bahamas for vacation," Calsa told them. "They've got a place there."

"What a liar." Maggie peered around the table, making sure she had everyone's attention. "She told me they were going to Utah, to a place called Snowbird, to go skiing. She said they have a chalet there. Can you beat that?"

Leo looked over at the table of black habits. "I wonder why Sister Alphonse didn't get to eat here."

"She never eats here," Maggie stated.

"I know that, stupid," said Leo. "I just thought they'd let her come, this being a special meal and all."

She looked back at Sister St. Paul's table. The only nuns who ate in the cafeteria were the ones who taught school. The others, who were older, ate in their own kitchen. From what she'd seen, it didn't seem like the two groups got along. She thought it had something to do with the new habits the teachers wore. Still, it was hard to tell, for the older nuns never talked much, and the only time she saw them, except for Sister Alphonse, was during mass. The rest of the time they hung out with Mother Superior in the convent section of the building, which was off limits to the students. Mother Superior was a mystery to her, too. The whole time she'd been there, Leo hadn't heard her say a word. She'd watched her praying during mass though, so she knew she could speak. The way she figured it, Mother Superior ran the show in the convent and Sister St. Paul ran the school.

"I don't see why they wouldn't let her come," Leo repeated. "I made a gimp necklace for her and everything."

Maggie snickered. "What's she going to do with that? Hang a whistle on it?"

"I thought she could put her keys on it, or a medal or something." Leo suddenly wondered if it was a good gift to give after all. She'd wanted to give Sister Alphonse something special. The nun was always saying nice things about her--told her she was a hard worker, that she did a good job. And about once a week Sister Alphonse would leave a brownie, or a pencil, or some other small treat in Leo's locker. That morning when she'd gone to the cleaning room to pick up her box she'd found Sister Alphonse kneeling on the floor, praying to her crucifix above the desk. Sister's face had been all shiny, and Leo had felt funny, like she shouldn't be there watching. The part that really bothered her though, was when the nun had tried to stand up. She'd had to use the desk, her knobby hands bracing her weight against the wood. She'd rushed to help her, and the nun had kept saying, 'Merci, merci,' until she'd finally gotten to her feet.

The more she thought about it, the angrier Leo became. Sister Alphonse was the nicest nun in the place and yet they gave her all the lousy jobs. She had to scrub the toilets and showers in the locker room, and burn all the trash. It wasn't right to make someone who couldn't even get up without the help of a desk, clean toilets on their hands and knees. If she was Sister Alphonse, she'd tell them where to go in a hurry, and why the nun didn't tell them, was something Leo couldn't understand.

After the drama club performed a short skit

portraying the birth of Christ, they left the cafeteria. The only good part of the play, as far as Leo was concerned, was Doris, who had dressed up like a donkey.

Once in the rec hall, they opened their gifts. Leo watched Marisa with great interest as the Mexican girl opened her pearl earrings. Marisa thanked her to the point where Leo got embarrassed and finally confessed that her mother had picked them out. Still, she couldn't help but boast, and told Marisa they'd come out of clams off the coast of Maine.

Carmine had gotten Leo's name and had knitted her a hat with matching mittens. The hat was navy blue and had a small gold anchor embroidered on it, like her captain's hat had had. Leo instantly put it on and paraded about for everyone to see.

Because Leo had already received a present, she was surprised when Hope cornered her near the tree and held a package out for her to take.

"Who's this from?" Leo asked.

"Me," said Hope.

"But I already got mine."

"This one's from me. I wanted you to have it."

"What is it?"

"Open it up and see."

Leo, still dumbfounded, opened the present. Her hand ran over the hard cover of the book--*The Adventures of Huckleberry Finn*, by Mark Twain.

"His real name was Samuel Clemens," said Hope. "My father gave that to me. I wanted you to have it. You remind me of the boy. You were the only one I could give it to."

"But if your father gave it to you, shouldn't you keep it?" Leo asked, not sure if she should accept it, but wanting to.

"I have to give it to someone, and you're the only one. . . It meant a lot to me. He gave it to me a long time ago. It's special. You'll like it. You're in it. Just like I used to be. Did I mention my father gave it to me?"

Leo nodded, wondering why Hope would give her the book if it meant that much to her. "Thanks Hope. I know I'll like it. I'll read it over vacation, then if you want, you can have it back."

"No, oh no, it's yours. Yours to keep. I'm giving it to you. You read all the time. I've watched you; you read *Lord Of The Flies*, three times."

Leo looked at her, amazed that Hope had noticed.

"I know you'll like it; Huck's just like you." Hope smiled, then walked off like she had something more important to do.

Leo looked down at the book. It's cover was a deep shade of red and each page was trimmed with a thin layer of gold. She hurried over to Maggie and tried to tell her how Hope had given her the book, but Maggie was too busy to listen. She and Calsa were laughing about the stuffed hippopotamus Doris had given her. It had a flower in its mouth and Calsa said it was probably a big seller in Fort Kent, where Doris was from.

When all the presents had been opened, everyone gathered in a circle and sang carols while

Sister Bernedette played the piano. Finally hoarse, they feasted on punch and cookies that were laid out beside Christmas napkins. When Sister St. Paul announced it was time for bed, even Leo was tired. Sister told them she hoped they all had a safe and Merry Christmas, and after they prayed the Our Father, the girls were hustled off to their dorms.

On the way upstairs, Leo overheard some of the girls saying the seniors were going to sing once the lights were out. She dismissed it as a lie, but when the lights were turned off, she heard voices in the hall.

All the girls sat up in bed, and those who slept in the alcoves turned back their green curtains to watch the procession. The seniors, dressed in long red nightgowns, entered the dark dorm, each carrying a tall candle and singing *Silent Night*. Leo thought they sounded like angels, their voices making her shiver as she clutched Cousin It, and watched in awe. They proceeded down one aisle and up the other, their candles flickering soft shadows with each footstep. When they left to sing for the other dorms, Leo fell back into bed. She rested her head on her pillow, her fingers searching beneath it until they touched the visor.

Late that night, Leo was shaken from sleep by the sound of urgent voices. The tone sent a nightmare chill through her, and she bolted upright, thinking, Dad's having a reaction.

There was a light on in Hope's alcove and the shadows, magnified behind the curtain, moved in a scary frenzy.

"Get Sister Martha. Have her call an ambulance. Hurry Calsa!"

Calsa shot out of the alcove and down the aisle. Leo threw her covers back and made it to the curtain in three strides. She brushed the cloth aside: Hope was lying on the bed, her eyes rolling in their sockets like marbles. Blood stained the sheets, the pillow, the floor, and was splattered across Sister Theresa's white nightgown.

"Go back to bed, Leona!"

Leo stood, feet rooted, eyes going from the towels wrapped around Hope's wrists, to the pale face, to the mouth whispering words she couldn't understand.

"Now!"

Sister's tone snapped Leo into motion. She ran back to her bed and perched on its edge, watching Sister's shadow. Then she heard racing footsteps pounding down the hall and Sister Martha flew past like a streak of light in the dark. In her hand she carried the first aid box. Calsa panted behind her. "Right there!" she said, pointing to Hope's alcove.

Others began to wake up, asking questions in dazed sleepy voices.

Maggie waved Calsa over. "What happened?"

Calsa crawled into bed beside Maggie, pulling the blankets around her with her good arm. "Get me warm, Maggie. I'm so cold."

"God, you're shaking."

"She cut her wrists, Maggie. She tried to kill herself."

"But why?" asked Leo, still watching the shadows behind the curtain.

Calsa shook her head. "I heard her groaning. Christ, I though she was sick."

"I thought Dad was having a reaction," said Leo. "I thought I had to get the insulin."

"Is she going to be all right?" Maggie whispered.

"I don't know. She used a razor blade. It's everywhere."

Maggie's voice shook. "What is?"

"Blood," Leo answered.

The dorm lights came on, the brightness jolting Leo like a scream. Sister St. Paul, wearing a white robe and no veil, ran ahead of two men with a stretcher. A third man carried a black bag and glass bottles.

The first thing Leo thought when she saw them rush by, was how odd Sister St. Paul looked with her hair showing. It was short, black, wavy.

When they carried Hope out, there were only two bandages around her wrists. Her arms were strapped over the blanket by her sides and she had a tube sticking out of the side of her neck--a rubber snake, running up to a glass bottle. It didn't seem possible to Leo that all that blood could have come from under those small bandages, and she wondered if Hope had cut herself someplace else, too.

The girls stood by their beds, some still not

knowing, but the whispers were flying, informing. All around her, the dorm buzzed with it.

Trying to cover her stained nightgown with a towel, Sister Theresa walked out of Hope's alcove, and quickly returned to her own. When she emerged a few minutes later, she was wearing her habit. "Everyone," she said in a voice so low, that Leo could barely hear her, "go back to bed."

Leo lay back, listening as Sister Martha and Sister Theresa cleaned up Hope's alcove. The strong smell of disinfectant made her eyes smart, her head hurt. Why would anyone with a name like Hope try to kill herself? Why would anyone? She buried her face in her pillow, tried to block out the strong odor, the water sounds. She kept seeing the blood, Hope's rolling eyes, Sister Theresa's face. Like a photograph, it stayed still--as still as that frozen moment.

When the nuns were finished cleaning, Sister Theresa, seeing that everyone was still awake, told them to kneel beside their beds and say a prayer for Hope. Leo felt the cold floor beneath her knees, thankful to feel some kind of pain. Grateful for the chance to help Hope.

Hands neatly folded for prayer, she bent her head and closed her eyes. But the words wouldn't come. How could she ask for His help when He'd let it happen? She remembered the red book, felt the urge to cry, but no tears came, just a wrenching feeling in her stomach like someone was pulling her insides out. *Why?* she asked him. *Why'd you let her do it?* Her name is Hope. If you let her die I'll hate you. I mean it. I'll hate you forever. Amen.

She crawled into her bed and stared up at the ceiling. If He let His own son die . . . Dear Jesus, she prayed, I know I'm supposed to ask your father for the big ones, but couldn't you help me? Just this one time? I promise I'll be good. I'll even forgive them for burning my hat. Please? Don't let Hope die. Amen, Leo.

She laid awake long after the nuns turned the lights out, her mind alert and wrestling with images of death: Father Richie's mother; Hope with all that blood. In the darkness it triggered a flashback of something long since buried--the day her mother came home from the hospital without the new baby. She watched the memory like a movie, saw the colors, felt the cold.

She was playing with her cocker spaniel, Taffy, sliding down a hill in an orange flying saucer. Then, they were in the driveway, the snowbanks taller than she was. She saw the red station wagon turn into the drive, stood with Taffy, waiting for it to stop. But the car didn't stop. It kept getting bigger. And bigger. Taffy jumped up on her, knocking her into a snowbank. Then her father was standing over her. He tried to pick her up, but she struggled free, kicking him with her boots. Taffy lay in front of the black tire with a red line across her open mouth. She crawled across the snow, patted the fur with her mitten, then took the mitten off. But Taffy wouldn't move. From above, her father kept saying dead, and she knew then what the word meant: Taffy would never play with her again. Knew then, why her baby sister was never coming home. She looked up, saw her mother standing still as a tree, her face different, white like the snow and wet with icy diamonds.

X.

CHRISTMAS EVE

The next morning at chapel, Sister St. Paul told them that the hospital had called--Hope was going to be all right. She said they would all need strength to get over the tragedy, and that Hope and her parents would need their prayers. After mass, no one talked about it. There were bags to finish packing, cars waiting, planes to catch. It was Christmas Eve, and everyone except the Mexicans were going home.

The drive to Portland was a cold one. Memere's heater wasn't working, but Leo didn't mind. After last night, she would have walked home barefoot if it meant getting out of there. She kept hashing the whole thing over in her mind but still hadn't found an answer as to why Hope would do that to herself. It had never occurred to her before that someone would actually try to kill themselves on purpose. She'd never even heard the word "suicide" until that morning at breakfast, or if she had, hadn't known what it meant. That Hope was the same age as Maggie, also caused her to worry. If Hope would do that, would her sister?

When they got to Portland, Memere took them downtown so they could do their Christmas shopping before going home. Congress Street was decked out in its traditional attire. But Leo hardly noticed the lighted red bells hugging lamp posts, or the tuffs of tinsel wrapped around telephone poles like silver snakes, or the endless strings of colored lights blinking gaily along the storefronts. If it had been twenty-fours hours sooner, she would have been full of wonder and excitement. And though she bought everyone in her family a gift, by the time she walked out of the 88 Cent Store, she'd forgotten what they were, and had to look in her bag in order to remember.

As soon as she walked through the front door of her house, the daze she'd been walking around in finally lifted. She was home. Safe. Everyone she loved lived there.

The house smelled of evergreen and baking, and was filled with her mother's warm laughter. Her father was supposed to arrive that evening and she knew that was the reason her mother was all dressed up. When she told her, "Boy, Ma, you look better than those ladies in the Sears catalog," her mother answered, "I wanted to look nice for once."

After hiding her presents, she followed her nose to the kitchen.

"What are you making, Mabel?" she asked, climbing onto one of the bar stools. "Sugar cookies?"

The big woman tried to camouflage a smile and told her, "Just one."

"Oh, come off it, Mabel, it's Christmas Eve. Can't you spare two for a starving child in Portland?"

"You!" Mabel bent over and kissed the top of Leo's head. "It's nice having you around. I miss you girls, the house ain't the same."

"Why don't you tell Ma that, then maybe she'd let me stay home." Leo decapitated an angel cookie, savoring its red sugar sprinkles.

"Your mother's business is your mother's business," Mabel responded.

"Aw, that's your answer to everything."

"Now, don't get fresh." She pointed the spatula at Leo. "Ain't they teaching you any manners at that school?"

"No. Fact is, I'm worse than before. Ma listens to you. She says even though you don't have an education, you're smarter than all of us put in one, or together, or something like that."

"You fibbing on the eve of the Lord's birthday?"

"No way, I'd have to go to confession again." Leo spun on her stool, then paused long enough to ask. "How much blood does a person got to loose before they die, Mabel?"

Mabel almost dropped the glass of milk she'd just poured. "What child?"

"How much blood do you have to loose before you die. You know, if you got cut or something."

"I don't know. What you have a fool question

like that in your head for?"

"Just do."

Mabel handed Leo her milk. "Well, that's nothing a girl your age should be worrying about."

Leo munched thoughtfully on another cookie, then asked, "Did Judas go to hell, Mabel?"

"My Lord, you're full of gems today."

"Did he? You know, 'cause he hanged himself after he ratted on Jesus?"

"Why don't you ask the nuns at school, you got a question like that?"

"'Cause I just thought of it." She frowned at Mabel. "I never wondered about him going to hell, though. I just figured he didn't 'cause, see if he didn't rat on Jesus, we'd never have Easter, and God couldn't put a guy in hell when He had the whole thing figured out all the time. Could He?"

Returning to the stove, Mabel told her, "I don't know how your head works, Leo. You better ask your mother."

Being a nurse, she'd probably know about the blood part, thought Leo. But how could she ask her mother that? She would want to know why. Besides, her mother seemed so happy about her father coming home, she didn't want to wreck it.

"There, your Momma has everything ready for tomorrow."

"You leave early today, Mabel?"

"Sure do. I got baking of my own. I'll be up all night."

"I wonder if Ma will leave cookies and milk out for Santa. She did last year. Only Mikey believes in him."

"Sometimes, it's good to do things even when you don't believe anymore. Keeps a body young at heart."

"What's young at heart mean?"

Mabel stood still for a moment, searching for an explanation. "It means, even though a body's old, they feel young inside."

Something about Mabel's definition struck her. It seemed to her that she was just the opposite. She was young on the outside, but inside, she felt older than Memere.

"Something bothering you, child?" Mabel asked her.

"No," Leo told her quickly, "nothing at all. . . It's just good to see you. It's just good to be home."

"Now look what you made me go and do," said Mabel, patting at a tear with the edge of her apron. "Dang, if you don't have the power to say nice things when you want to." Mabel took the plate of cookies and held it out for Leo. "Now grab a couple and scat before I change my mind."

Leo walked into the main hall and planted herself on the hassock. Munching on a cookie, she studied the tree across from her trying to imagine its branches dressed in lights and ornaments. It was nice of her brothers to wait for her and Maggie, she thought. It wouldn't have been the same if they'd decorated the tree without them. The tree was smaller than the year before. The last few years her mother had gotten into the habit of saying, "This is going to be a small Christmas--this year we're getting a smaller tree." She figured if her mother kept saying that, by the time she was Mark's age, they would have to put the tree on a table or they might trip over it.

She wiped the cookie crumbs off her pant legs, then wandered into the living room. A fire burned in the fireplace, their empty red stockings above it. She could tell Mark had done the cleaning because the furniture was moved around. Her mother had told her Mark had a concert to play at, and when he got home, they'd decorate the tree.

She rolled up into a ball on the couch and from her fetal position, looked at the touches of Christmas: red candles in brass holders, a poinsettia, a laughing Santa statue. Tomorrow, this room would be full of toys. Each chair would have a stocking on it and a pile of unwrapped presents. The toys would be put together, have batteries, be all ready to play with. The wrapped presents under the tree were never opened until after Christmas dinner. But she didn't care, they were always clothes.

She glared at the red leather chair, remembering the Christmas when all she'd asked for was a G.I. Joe Bazooka gun. On Christmas morning she'd run down the stairs, and there it was, sitting in the red chair. She'd never bothered to look at the stocking beside it, she'd just assumed it was hers, and was in the process of wiping out whole armies with her new gun when her parents came downstairs. She'd been broken hearted when her mother had told her the Bazooka gun wasn't hers, it was her brother's. Instead of a gun she'd gotten a walking doll as tall as she was.

She looked away from the chair. The only time she'd ever played with that stupid walking doll was when she'd taken its eyes out with a screwdriver to see what made them open and close.

Feeling drowsy, her head full of Christmas past, she recalled the year Maggie had gotten marionette puppets and cried all day about it. And the time Hal knocked the tree over going out for a pass. And how their dog, Sukey had thought just because it was a tree it was all right to pee under it. But even with her recollections, and the fire, and the smell of the tree, Christmas didn't seem as important as it used to.

Maggie entered the room brushing out her wet hair. "You wrap your presents yet?"

Leo shook her head.

"You'd better get it done. Christmas is tomorrow."

"Big deal."

Maggie sat down on the couch beside her. "Did you tell Ma?"

Leo looked at her. "No. Did you?"

"I didn't want to spoil things."

"Me neither."

"Are you going to?" Maggie questioned. "I mean sometime?"

Leo looked away. "Like the Old Man says, 'what she don't know, won't hurt her.'"

Hal walked into the room wearing a big grin and rosy cheeks. "When did you get home?"

"A little while ago," Leo told him. "Memere

took us downtown so we could do our shopping."

"Dad home yet?" he asked, shaking off his coat.

"Nope," said Leo. "Ma said he ain't coming till tonight."

"I hope he gets home before I leave." Hal playfully threw a glove at Leo. "I got a hot date."

"Who now?" asked Maggie.

"No one I'd want you to know." Hal made his eyebrows dance. "But she has a car."

"I bet that's the only reason you're gong out with her," said Leo.

"Hey, it's winter, what can I say?" Hal flopped down into the red chair. "But that's not the only reason I've given her the privilege of going out with me."

Maggie pegged a pillow at him. "Spare us."

Hal started laughing. "I wouldn't do that if I were you; it took the Interior Decorator an hour to decide where to put that." Then he looked at Leo with his laughing blue eyes and demanded, "What'd you get me for Christmas?"

"Nothing," Leo told him.

"Good," he laughed. "I got you the same thing."

Memere brought down her presents," Maggie snickered. "I'll give you three guesses."

"Pajamas, pajamas, and pajamas," Hal replied.

"Remember the ones she made me last year" Maggie laughed. "The ones with the big orange giraffes on them?"

"Maybe this year they'll have hippos on them to match your stuffed animal." Leo jumped off the couch to avoid Maggie's punch.

"Just for that I'm taking your present back," Maggie told her, then turning to Hal, said, "She did her shopping at the 88 Cent Store again."

"Oh, no!" cried Hal. "Chocolate covered cherries! Remember those? They were so petrified the dog wouldn't even eat them."

Leo laughed all the way up the stairs, recalling what a bargain those cherries had been at four boxes for eight-eight cents. When she entered her room she almost tripped over Mikey. He was sitting on the floor looking like he'd just lost his best friend.

"What are you doing?" she asked.

"Thinking," Mikey replied.

"About what?"

"About how I don't have n-no presents for n-no one."

Leo sat down beside him, and thought for a second herself. "I know what you can give," she finally told him.

"What?" he asked, not sounding hopeful.

"Come with me." Leo got up and led her brother over to her closet, then rattled around inside until she found the shoe box.

"What's that?" asked Mikey.

Leo lifted the lid carefully, as if something fragile were inside. From the box she took a gold tie-tac with the initial M etched on it. "See this? I found it in the couch when I was looking for money once. It's Mark's favorite one." She handed it to Mikey. "I bet if you gave it back to him all wrapped up, he'd be so happy it would be better than buying him a new one."

A look of astonishment lit up Mikey's face. "Think so?"

"Know so. And here, look." She held up a small heart-shaped barrette with two tiny rhinestones in it. "This is Maggie's. I found it in the bathroom under the tub a long time ago. See those jewels? They're diamonds. It's the same kind they have in Queen's crowns."

"Could I g-give it back to Maggie for a present?" he asked, catching on.

"You're getting the idea," Leo told him. "See, this box is full of stuff that everyone's lost and I've found. Like this, Hal's I.D. bracelet. Remember how he looked all over for it? Well, I found it in the garage by the window. He must have taken it off to play basketball and forgot."

"How c-come you didn't give it to him?"

"He never offered a reward, silly." She took a silk scarf from the box and held it up to her nose. "This is Ma's. Here take a whiff. Smells like her, don't it?"

Mikey took a sniff and nodded.

"I want to keep this," Leo told him, putting it back. "But I have something else you can give her." She took out a tiny bottle of perfume. "Came all the way from Paris, France. Says so, right there. It's French, and Ma likes anything that's French. Especially when it smells like a million Lilies of the Valley." She held it out for him to take.

"B-but it's almost gone," he said, showing her the near empty bottle.

"Oh, that's okay. All we got to do is fill it up with water and it will look brand new."

"Wow," said Mikey, excitedly. "Ma loves smelly stuff."

Leo pawed through the other odds and ends in her box, then took out a corn cob pipe with teeth marks on the end. "You can give Dad this. It's almost new. Hardly chewed on. You know how he likes to eat them. He must of set it on the sun porch railing and it got knocked off 'cause I found it in the lilac bushes. You know how he's always putting his pipes on things and forgetting about them. Anyhow, it's so new, it's hardly black inside."

"Can I really have these?" Mikey looked down at his haul.

"Sure, I said you could, didn't I? I'll even help you wrap them decent."

Mikey fingered Mark's tie-tac, then took another sniff of the perfume. "I wish I was as smart as you."

"When you get my age, you will be."

By the time she was finished wrapping her and Mikey's presents, Mabel had left and Mark had gotten home. He was in the main hall arranging strings of lights, checking each one for burned out bulbs.

"Hi, Mark," she called, as she and Mikey scrambled down the stairs.

"C-can we do the tree now?" asked Mikey,

152

touching one of the dead bulbs.

"Wash your hands first," Mark told him. "You can't touch the ornaments unless you have clean hands."

Mikey raced off toward the bathroom, and Leo sat down on the bottom step, watching Mark replace bulbs. She noticed he'd lined them up so no two lights of the same color were next to each other. "How'd your concert go?" she asked him.

Mark looked up at her. "I never made a mistake. I wish Ma could have heard me."

Leo wasn't surprised, Mark never made mistakes, even when he was practicing. She loved listening to him play the piano. "I wish I could have heard you, too. Were there many people there?"

"There weren't enough seats. It was packed... Afterward, everyone else left with their parents to go out to eat, and I walked home. Should have worn my heavy coat, it's freezing out."

"Are you going to Midnight Mass?" she asked.

Mark put his hands out in front of him, moved his fingers over the keys of an invisible piano. "I was great." Then he glanced up at his sister. "I don't know if I will or not. I've got to work from six to nine."

"The department store's open on Christmas Eve?"

Mark nodded. "They make the part-timers work all the crummy hours."

The doorbell rang and Leo jumped up. "Maybe it's Dad!"

"Hello, Leo! Merry Christmas!" Their Aunt Bo

from Boston stood on the steps with her arms full of presents. "Aren't you going to let me in? It's colder than Alaska out here."

Leo opened the door and helped her aunt carry the gifts inside.

"Hello, Mark! Boy, the house looks nice," said Aunt Bo, glancing around. "You haven't decorated the tree yet?"

"They waited for me and Maggie to get home."

Mikey, Hal, and Maggie, hearing their aunt's voice, joined them in the hall.

"Merry Christmas, Aunt Bo," said Hal in a deep voice. "You're looking beautiful, as usual." Hal gave her a big kiss and hug.

"And you're still full of malarkey," she told him, then reached for Mikey. "Come here, Mikey, you look good enough to eat." She gathered him up, lifting him right off the floor.

"I can't breath," Mikey croaked.

Aunt Bo's big laugh rolled out, and her whole body jiggled. Their Aunt Bo was even bigger than Mabel and always said she liked being big because there was more for her kids to love. By, "her kids," she meant the children she had for patients at the hospital. Most of them were poor, and terminally ill. Once, when Leo asked her why she didn't have any kids of her own, she'd told her, "I do; I have so many, I can't count them all."

With their aunt's help, they decorated the tree. Aunt Bo sang carols as she worked, and in between songs, showered them with compliments, asked them questions about school, work, what they'd been up to. Aunt Bo had a way of making them talk about things they usually wouldn't. She even got Mark to play a piece on the piano, something he rarely did for anyone.

The tree looked as beautiful as Leo had imagined it would. The lights looked like huge, colored tear drops in warm reds, royal blues, kelly greens, and pale whites. The angel at the top was the same one they'd had every year. It was a gift to their parents the first year they'd been married. It had fine, feather silk wings, and was the last thing they put on the tree.

"It's beautiful. Just beautiful," said Aunt Bo, stepping back to admire their work. "And look at all those presents! My poor kids wouldn't know what to do with so much. You don't realize how lucky you are." She shook her head slowly. "It looks like Santa Claus already came."

"No, he didn't," Mikey told her. "He comes tonight."

"That's right." She grabbed and hugged him again. "When you're fast asleep. What's he bringing you this year?"

Mikey looked up at her, then said softly, "M-my daddy. That's all I-I asked for."

Later that evening, Leo sat with her mother and Mikey in the living room, listening to Bing Crosby and watching the fire. Mark had gone to work,

Maggie had left to visit Ellen, and Hal had gone out on his hot date with the car. She knew her mother wasn't happy about them not being home for their father's arrival, but inside, Leo was glad they weren't--it was nice having her mother all to herself.

She looked over at Mikey, who had tried to stay awake. They had covered him up with a blanket and all Leo could see of his head was a small tuft of blonde hair.

Her mother got up and checked out the window for the hundredth time. "Here comes a car," she said, then with disappointment added, "And there it goes."

Leo watched her pace across the carpet. This is probably how she acted that Easter, thought Leo, probably hung around the window waiting for us to come home. On Easter, a few years back, Leo's father had taken them visiting while her mother stayed home preparing dinner. He'd taken them up to her grandfather's for a visit and after, to a relative's she'd never met before or at least hadn't remembered. He'd started drinking there, and didn't stop until Mark went out and sat in the car. On their way home, at the rotary with the huge anchor in the center, her father had lost control of the car. The station wagon careened over the curb, onto the grass and stopped a few inches from the steel anchor which was three times the size of the car. Her father got out and, to her horror, left them there. By the time he came back with a tow truck, Hal had taken off to a friend's who lived nearby, Mark was laying in the back seat praying no one he knew would see him, and she, Maggie and Mikey were sitting on the anchor. It was five o'clock when they'd finally gotten home. Dinner was ruined and her mother was hysterical, saying over and over, how she'd been worried sick.

But that's how most holidays went for them. They would start out good, but by the end of the day, turn into something else. Usually by suppertime her father was either drunk or on his way to having a diabetic reaction. There weren't too many times they'd gotten through a holiday without a fight or something happening--somehow the day would eventually get spoiled. It was almost expected. Knowing that, she wondered if this Christmas would be any different.

"Ma?"

"Mmm?"

"Do you think Dad will look any different?"

Her mother turned away from the window and stared at her. "What do you mean?"

Leo hedged. "I don't know."

Her mother walked across the room to where Leo was sitting, and gently brushed the bangs from her face. "If you mean will he act any different, we'll just have to wait and see."

Leo leaned her face against her mother's hand and felt the sudden urge to tell her everything--about Hope, and Father Richie's mother, and how she was afraid to believe that her father would really stop drinking. But they both heard a car stop, and her chance to tell was gone.

Her mother hurried into the hall, straightening

her dress as she went. The front door opened and her father, carrying his suitcase and a big, flat, rectangular package, walked in. She stood back as her parents embraced. They were usually careful about getting mushy in front of her, but they didn't seem to know she was there. She watched her father's crippled hands rub the back of her mother's navy dress, saw him bury his face in her hair, and heard him say, "I missed you so much."

She felt awkward, as though she didn't belong there, felt perhaps, they'd rather be alone and started to walk back into the living room.

"Leo?"

She turned and looked at her father, who still had his arm around her mother. "Hi, Dad."

"Thanks for all the letters," he told her. "It's nice to get mail."

Especially on your birthday, she thought. "Yeah, it is."

"How's school?"

Hope tried to kill herself last night. "Fine, thanks."

"I showed everyone at the hospital your report card. All A's . . . You're getting as smart as your brother."

His name's Mark and there's nothing to do there but study. "I got a B in math, remember?"

"It's still a big improvement. I'm proud of you." Her father looked down at his shoes, then back at her as though he were running out of things to say. "Do I get a kiss? Or are you too old for that?"

I'm older than Memere, she thought, but

hesitantly walked over to her father and let him hug her.

"I'm sorry for a lot of things, Leo. I just wanted you to know that."

She stepped away from him, studied the face that seemed strange to her. Did he mean it, she wondered. Was it from his heart?

For a moment no one said anything, then he looked around expectantly. "The tree looks nice . . . Where is everyone?"

Her mother touched his hand, explaining. "They're not here. They waited as long as they could. Mark had to work, Maggie's at Ellen's and Hal's out. Mikey's in there sleeping. He tried his best to stay awake."

Her father walked into the living room and Leo watched him stand over Mikey. Carefully, he tucked the blanket around Mikey's feet, then rejoined them in the hall. "He's grown," he said, then picked up his suitcase, leaving the present behind. "I'll bring this upstairs."

Leo stood by her mother, watching him move up the steps, and deep inside, she felt something stir.

"I'll be upstairs," her mother told her. "I think he'd like to talk to me alone for awhile, okay honey?"

"Sure, go ahead. Maggie will be home soon, anyhow. We're going to get ready for mass."

Leo watched her mother go, then returned to the living room and collapsed into the red chair. The house was so quiet she could hear Mikey sighing in his sleep. She looked over at him, remembering how carefully her father had tucked the blanket around him, how sad his voice had sounded when he'd said, "He's grown." Guilt gnawed at her, left her more confused than ever. Why hadn't she been happy to see him? Why had she felt mad?

She looked around the room as though searching for the answer, her gaze resting on the statue of the Little King. He was dressed in the red silk robes of Christmas, and the rubies in his crown looked like drops of blood in the dim light. The Little King was suppose to be Jesus, and had different clothes for different Holy days. Her mother had dressed him in black after President Kennedy was shot. In one hand, he held a world with a cross on top of it, his other hand was raised, with two fingers ready to bless. The Little King stood inside a glass dome and whenever anyone had extra money, they were suppose to put it under the globe by his feet. When enough money was collected, her parent's donated it to the Nuns of the Precious Blood. No one was ever suppose to steal from the Little King. If they did, something terrible would happen. She knew it was true--she'd done it. She'd stolen a nickel once to buy a marshmallow heart, and that very night her parents had gotten into a big fight over her father's drinking. It was all her fault: she'd taken the nickel and the Little King was punishing her for it. For a long time afterward, she'd thought it was her fault that her father drank.

She looked back at Mikey, at the blanket tucked in with love. Tonight was the first time she'd seen her father without a drop of Vodka in him. Tonight she had met her real father, someone who showed off her report card, someone who said he was proud of her. Maybe she was mad because he could have been that someone all along.

Walking to Midnight Mass was like stepping into a wonderland. The falling snow stuck to telephone wires, fences, branches, and parked cars. It made Leo feel as though she were inside one of those Christmas balls with the figures in them, the kind you could shake up, then watch the fake snow float through the water like a blizzard.

Leo stomped behind Maggie and her two brothers in boots that were too big--her mother had gotten them on sale, and Hal said he could see why. She watched him and Mark walking ahead of her, the snow clinging to their coats. Mark's, was camel hair: Hal's was what Maggie called a "Surplus Store Special." Hal couldn't care less what he wore and looked good in anything. Mark would only wear brand names, and in his closet, always hung his shirts in the same direction. It's a wonder they get along at all, she thought.

Before they'd left for mass, her father had come down to say hello. They'd all stood in the hall saying polite things to each other, "You look great Dad" . . . "School's fine, thanks" . . . "Yes, I've got money for church" . . . "That's right, it's snowing" . . . "We'll see you later, Dad" . . . "It's good to have you home."

Her father had even told Mark that the house looked great. It had just about knocked her over.

By the time they got to church, Leo couldn't feel her legs. She walked behind Hal as he led them down the aisle to a pew near the front.

"After you, little sister." Hal stepped aside so Leo could enter the pew first.

She didn't like the smirk on Hal's face, and when she looked into the pew, she balked. Jack was kneeling there with his parents. He was wearing a pea coat like Hal's and had let his hair grow longer, but otherwise he looked the same.

"Merry Christmas," whispered Hal, nudging her.

She knelt down beside Jack, while Hal made a big deal about shaking Jack's father's hand, and telling his mother how lovely she looked.

Closing her eyes, she tried to pray, but could feel Jack watching her. He'd never written to her once. He can take the short road to hell, she thought, and take that Nancy what's her face with him.

Through the entire High Mass as Father McBrady wailed in Latin and the choir chipped in their responses, she tried to ignore Jack. Still, her eyes occasionally wandered, her gaze resting on his hands and the scars that crisscrossed the skin like a road map: a constant reminder of a cherry bomb gone bad, a prank that had almost killed him, one he would remember every time he looked in a mirror with no shirt on--the skin about his neck drawn tight like an old man's wrinkles, his chest raised and rubbery with skin grafts. It had happened before she really knew him. She thought if it hadn't happened, he would have been too cool to ever know her.

On their way out of church, Jack caught up with her. "You mad at me or something?" he asked, touching her elbow.

She looked down at his hand, at the scars she'd grown used to. "Why should I be?"

"I don't know, but I have the feeling you are."

"I ain't mad at you, Jack. It's the rest of the world."

"That's good to know," he laughed softly. "By the way, Hal told me about your hat. It was a shitty thing for them to do."

She stared up at him, and the caring look in his blue eyes made her want to cry.

"Can I walk you home?" he asked.

"Sure," she told him, "it's a free country."

As she and Jack walked up Cragie Street, she looked ahead at the three dark figures of Maggie, Mark, and Hal. They crested the hill and disappeared, and she wondered briefly how they felt about their father's homecoming, if the politeness had driven them crazy, too.

She shuffled along beside Jack, her boots swimming around her cold feet, and just as they passed the Browns, whose house was ablaze in blue Christmas lights that threw shadows across the snow, she told him about Hope.

It came out as softly as the falling snow, and Jack listened to it all, his head bent downward, as if to hear her better. The walls she'd built to protect herself had finally cracked under the weight of heavy burdens, and through that fissure the pressure was released. She'd told someone who cared and who wouldn't be hurt by listening.

XI.

VOICE OF DEMOCRACY

Leo moved through the water, breathing with every other stroke. All week, she'd spent two hours each day practicing with the Seals. She could feel her coach watching, could picture him sitting on the bench, his glasses on the tip of his nose, his arms crossed over his big belly. She liked him, even feared him a little. She wanted to show him she was still good. She wouldn't stop to rest, though her lungs were burning, her legs and arms weak. This was where she belonged and she was grateful to be here--she wouldn't stop until she'd finished a mile.

To take her mind off the pain, she thought about her father. He'd left on Tuesday and hadn't taken a drink, though he'd had a chance to. A friend of his named Joe Roma had stopped by for a visit. He'd been living in Alaska and hadn't seen her father in ten years. He'd brought him a bottle of liquor in a pretty box decorated with old cars and a red bow. When the man left, she heard her father tell Hal that

Joe Roma was a skirt chaser from way back, and that he used to call him Roaming Joe. She'd watched her father hold the bottle, turning it in his hands, heard him say, "It'd be a shame to waste it." But then he handed it to Hal and said, "Take it and dump it in a snowbank. Some lucky pigeon will have a Merry Christmas."

The black lines in the Boy's Club pool were fatter than Kiwanis, and the bottom was made up of thousands of tiny square tiles. It was only a four lane-pool, twenty-five yards instead of meters. She did a flip turn and started toward the other end.

Mikey had caught on fast to the gift-giving scheme, presenting her with a bag of her own marbles. The best present of the day was her father's gift to her mother. It was a painting he'd done at the hospital. The frame was the same color as Old Orchard sand. It was an ocean scene--breaking waves against jagged rocks, sky a mixture of orange and blue light. It was beautiful; it made her feel like she was there watching those curling waves. Her mother had cried, said that's where Maggie got her artistic talent. Leo hadn't even known her father could paint.

She counted her strokes, stretched on her glide. Her coach had to be watching, noticing she hadn't let up, hadn't stopped. Through the water she could see the legs of those who had stopped, those holding onto the edge of the pool. They'd been practicing all winter, had been in meets right along. She'd show them. She picked up her pace.

During the three days her father was home there

wasn't one fight, but there was tension. Everyone was trying so hard to act like a normal family that the effort wore them out. She'd noticed that her father seemed almost relieved when it was time for him to return to the hospital.

The night her father left, Hal came home drunk. She'd been up reading *Huckleberry Finn*, and had gone down to the kitchen for a snack, when he'd come sneaking in the back door. She knew before he even said a word. She could see it in his red eyes, his walk, could smell him from across the room. The lucky pigeon told her not to tell, said he'd only had a couple of brews with the Pharmacy Boys, no big deal. She was worried. Hal had reminded her too much of her father.

Someone grabbed her arm to stop her. The other swimmer pointed toward their coach. Everyone was getting out of the pool, sitting on the deck for a lecture.

"Leo," came the gruff voice of her coach. "You stay in the water."

Leo shook the water out of her ears and pulled down her cap, watching the others gather. Finally, her coach told her, "I want you to do a fifty sprint. Freestyle. And start off the wall, Leo."

She looked at the other end of the pool. On the wall there was a huge outline of a champagne glass with the words, "This Water Is Fit To Drink," written beneath it. She inhaled deeply, felt the "rush" as she psyched herself up. She would do this one for her father, for not taking the drink she could tell he'd wanted.

She sprinted down the pool, taking no breaths. She felt light, relaxed, strong. She did a flip turn, stretched toward home. Midway down the pool she poured it on and didn't let up until her fingers hit hard against the wall.

That felt great, she thought. She stood up and turned toward her coach, her breath still coming in gasps.

"What you've just seen," said her coach, "is a girl who, up until this week, hasn't been in a pool since last summer." He paused and re-crossed his arms. "Now, she's bussed across town every morning for the past five days. Just to swim. How many of you have made it to practice every day this week?" He paused again, repositioning his glasses. "She not only came to practice, she managed to keep up with most of you who swim here year round. She just swam a thirty-two flat off the wall after swimming almost a mile. You saw her." The coach cleared his throat. "Now, I've been sitting up here the past hour, watching her and asking myself, how can she do it? How can she keep that pace up when my other swimmers, who work out every week, can't do it without taking a rest? Does anyone here think they know the answer?" The room remained silent and he continued. "Well, I'll tell you how. It's because she *wants* to do it. She *wants* to be good. She wants to beat all of you. Even more important, she wants to beat herself. And that, people, makes a competitor. She's made of the stuff it takes. And though I'm sorry she can't be on the team year round, I don't think I'm as sorry as she is. Am I right, Leo?"

Leo, embarrassed by the praise but loving every word of it, looked down at the water and nodded.

"Now, we've got twenty minutes left. Why don't you all get in the pool and show me you've got what it takes, too."

Talking with Jack on Christmas Eve had helped lighten the load, and the fissure had mended itself. Within the walls Leo's questions about Hope and her confused feelings about her father still waited for answers--but quietly.

Hope didn't come back after Christmas and the alcove across from Leo remained empty. All of Hope's belongings had been removed by the nuns, every trace of her erased--except from Leo's memory.

She'd heard rumors that the reason Hope tried to kill herself was because her parent's were getting a divorce. Even though Leo knew she'd be sad if her parents ever got divorced, she'd never kill herself over it, and felt there had to be another reason Hope had done what she'd done. She knew Sister St. Paul was right about Hope needing their prayers, and for a while Leo worried that without Hope being there and with all of her things gone, they'd forget that. It was a worry that didn't go away until she placed a small cardboard sign by the foot of the Jesus statue in the chapel. It read: Remember To Pray For Hope.

The days and weeks slipped into each other and

Leo went through the motions of school unnoticed--almost. After catching her reading *Goldfinger*, Sister St. Paul threw the James Bond book in the trash, where Leo had found it in the first place. Another time she'd hauled Leo into her office for starting a joke about Sister Bernedette. The nun had fallen down half a flight of stairs after Maggie scared her. Maggie had been caught out of bed after "lights out," and as punishment, Sister Theresa had made her sit in the hall in the dark. Sister Bernedette was walking up the stairs and hadn't bothered to turn the light on; she also hadn't expected Maggie to be sitting there. When Maggie went, "Boo!" Sister Bernedette went tumbling down the stairs. Hence, the joke: "What's black and white and red all over? Sister Bernedette falling down the stairs."

There was also potential trouble ahead. It began with a letter Evette wanted to send her boyfriend without having the nuns read it. Leo had offered to mail it for her, thinking she could give it to Angie to mail on her way home from school. One thing led to another and before she knew it she was smuggling out between five and ten letters a week for a handful of seniors. She and Angie split the profits of twenty-five cents a letter, and called their scam "The Pony Express." Leo justified their enterprise by making it a cause, and told Angie, "This is America, and no one has the right to read someone's mail, unless that someone wants them to."

❖ ❖ ❖ ❖

Every year at St. Christopher's a "Voice Of Democracy" speech contest was held for grades five through eight. Leo hadn't been too interested about it until Sister Marie mentioned trophies. Being a natural competitor, with two shelves full of ribbons, medals, and trophies for swimming, she automatically set her mind to winning the contest for her grade. Exerting the same drive that helped her win in the pool, she began working on her speech that same afternoon, and had just written her first paragraph when Doris appeared in the doorway.

"Leo, Maggie, phone call. Long distance."

Leo raced down the hall, trying to get to the phone first, but just as she reached for it, Maggie pushed her out of the way and grabbed the receiver. "Hello?" Maggie gasped.

Leo danced impatiently. It bugged her that Maggie always got to talk first. But this time, Maggie was quiet--hadn't said a thing besides "Hello."

"What's the matter?" Leo asked.

"Shhh!" Maggie told her. "I can't hear."

The expression on Maggie's face told her something was wrong. "Tell me," Leo demanded.

Maggie took the phone from her ear. "Ma says Nick was killed in Vietnam." Maggie turned back to the phone. "What Ma? She's right here, I'll put her on."

Leo took the phone, the news still sinking in. "Is it true, Ma? Is Nick really dead?"

Her mother's voice sounded as though it were further away than Portland. "Yes, Honey, I'm afraid it is."

"I want to come home."

"Leo, it will take a few weeks before they have the funeral. They've got to. . . It will just be awhile."

"I want to see Jack."

"I'll tell you what, when they have the funeral, you can come home for a few days. You can see Jack then. But I'd rather you didn't go to the services. I don't think it's a place for children."

Leo thought of Father Richie's mother and shivered. "I don't want to pay respects, Ma. I just want to see Jack."

"I'll have Memere pick you up when the time comes."

"Promise?"

"I promise. Now could you put Maggie back on? And Leo?"

"Yeah?"

"I love you."

"Me, too . . . Ma?"

"Yes, Leo, what is it?"

"What about Mark? He's almost as old as Nick and . . ."

"Mark's not going anywhere but college. He's already been accepted at Georgetown."

"But what about Hal?"

"Don't worry about your brothers, Leo; leave it to me. They'll never fight in this war."

"Okay, Ma, if you say so . . . I'll see you when I get home." Leo handed Maggie the phone, then walked off toward the rec hall. How could her mother be so sure her brothers would never have to fight? Jack's parents probably thought the same thing about Nick, and now he was dead. She sat by the window, the walls inside beginning to tremble. She tried to picture Nick, but the image kept getting blurred. She thought about Jack and how she'd feel if it were Mark or Hal. She wanted to go home, wanted to hug her brothers.

It didn't seem real that Nick was dead. Every night she sat beside Evette watching the T.V. war on the news, but all those numbers hadn't meant anything--they were about someone else, no one she knew; they didn't have faces; they didn't live down the street from her. The truth was, she didn't even know what the war was about. Until now, it hadn't involved her; it was just something on the news every night, just something going on.

Normally, the military click of Sister St. Paul's footsteps would have brought Leo to attention, but she continued to stare straight ahead into the afternoon light that slanted through the windows. I know what those numbers mean now, she thought. Each one of them are a Nick.

"I just talked with your mother," said Sister St. Paul.

The nun placed a hand on Leo's shoulder and Leo brushed it away. "Just leave me alone."

"I just wanted to say I'm sorry, Leona."

Leo looked up at her, searching the nun's face for the truth. "You should be," she said. "Everybody should."

❖ ❖ ❖ ❖

Three weeks later, Memere came and brought them home. Leo's mother and older brothers had gone to the funeral that morning, and when Leo got home, her mother told her it was all right to go over to Jack's house. She dressed up in her best jumper and good coat, wanting to look nice for him when she said she was sorry, then she walked the two familiar blocks.

For awhile she just stood at the end of Jack's driveway. She'd wanted to see him ever since her mother had told her the news, but now that she was here, she couldn't walk up to the front door. She glanced around at all the cars--it looked like a party.

"Are you coming in?"

The question startled her. Jack's father was standing in the doorway. She moved toward him, unsure of what to say. She had only prepared herself to tell Jack she was sorry. "Hello Mr. Burgess, I'm . . . I'm . . ."

Jack's father nodded as though he knew what she was trying to say. "It's nice of you to come, Leo," he said. "I saw your mother and your brothers at church this morning. Please thank them for me, will you?"

"I will," she promised, then followed him inside. The room was full of people. Jack's mother was sitting in a chair, acting like the room was empty. Leo watched her completely ignore Mrs. Gordon, who was flapping around her like an injured

bird. She'd never seen Jack's mother look that way.
She was always smiling. "Where's Jack?" Leo
asked his father.

"He's out on the back porch, I think. Would you
like something to eat, Leo?"

"I'm not hungry much, thanks."

"Why don't you go and find him, then. He'll be
glad you came."

Jack's father looked old, tired; he had dark spots
under his red-rimmed eyes.

"Are you okay, Leo?" he asked her.

"Sure. I'll just go out and see if I can find him."

She moved through the room full of grownups,
mostly neighbors who she knew. On the dining
room table, sitting beside a folded flag, was a picture
of Nick in his uniform. There were sandwiches,
brownies, and pastries surrounding it. It looked as
though Nick were watching the people get their
food. It gave her a strange feeling, as if she were
floating, as though her feet were off the floor and
she were looking down on the room from above.
Looking down from the ceiling, watching the people
move around the table for their food. She finally
made her way through the crowded kitchen where,
to her horror, she'd counted three men laughing.

Jack was sitting on the second step with his face
in his hands, elbows on his knees. He turned at the
sound of the door closing and looked up at her.

"I was wondering if you'd come. I saw your
brothers and your mom this morning, but I didn't get
to ask them if you were home."

Leo sat down beside him. "They let me out of

school."

"Is it any better?"

"Hope never came back. Other than that, it's the same--every time the bell rings you got to do something."

She looked around the backyard at the rusting swing set and the bare weeping willow, feeling awkward. Like that day with Father Richie, Leo wasn't sure of what she was suppose to say-- somehow "sorry" didn't seem enough, even if it was from her heart. She reached out and touched Jack's hand, running a tender finger across the swollen scars.

Jack rubbed the back of her fingers with his own. "You've got small hands," he said.

"I've got small feet, too. These boots are way too big, but Ma says I'll grow into them. Seems like I'm always waiting to grow into something."

"I used to hate getting Nick's hand-me-downs . . . I wouldn't now, you know?"

Leo gave an understanding nod. For awhile they sat in silence, still holding hands, each lost to their own troubled thoughts. After hearing about Nick, Leo had tried her best to discover what the war was about. Sister Marie had told her the people in North Vietnam were Communists, and they were trying to take over the whole country. She'd said the United States was over there to stop the spread of Communism, to help the people in South Vietnam fight for Democracy. It had taken Leo a long time to find Vietnam on the globe in her classroom. The country was so small its name barely fit inside of it.

She figured if the Communists wanted a place that was so small it took an hour to find it on the globe, then maybe the United States should just let them have it.

"I remember how he used to do flips off that swing set," said Jack, looking in its direction. He wiped at his eyes, not seeming to care that Leo could see him crying. "Christ, he's all over the house. Everywhere I look, I see him."

"I felt that way after Sukey died," Leo said quietly. "Her leash, her bed. A year after she died, Mabel moved the couch in the living room and there was one of her favorite balls. When she moved the couch back, I put the ball back under it again. It made it seem like Sukey was still around in a way. Was that a stupid thing to do, Jack? I never told anyone 'cause I thought they'd think it was queer."

Jack sighed and cleared his throat. "I got one of Nick's shirts under my pillow because it smells like him. See, I never even got to touch him again. They had this glass thing over his casket so we wouldn't get any diseases. The shirt's as close as I'm gonna get."

Leo nodded again, knowing nothing she could say would take the hurt out of Jack's voice. She stayed with him the rest of the afternoon, and though later she wouldn't be able to recall much of what they talked about, she remembered some things. Like how Jack said his parents got a letter from Nick two days before his wake, saying he'd be home for his birthday in July. Or how Jack never let go of her hand the whole time they sat together on the porch steps. Or how deep inside, she couldn't help feeling glad it wasn't Mark or Hal.

Sunday morning Leo sat in the kitchen watching her mother prepare the noon meal. The sun came through the window in wide rays, a beam of light falling on her mother's bent head as she peeled potatoes. Leo listened to the scraping of the knife, the soft landing of peelings. The house was still; everyone else was at ten o'clock mass.

"You got up early for mass," said her mother. "Why didn't you sleep in while you had the chance?"

"I like the seven o'clock mass. It's shorter." She'd also wanted to get it over with so she could be home.

"Do you have your things packed yet?"

Leo sighed, leaning her chin on her hand. "No."

"That was quite a sigh. What's the matter?"

She wanted to say, I don't want to go back, I want to stay home with you, stay right here in this chair and watch you peel potatoes for the rest of my life. But instead she offered one of her father's explanations: "Life in general."

Her mother placed a potato in the bowl, shook the water from her hands, then picked up another spud to peel. "You haven't said anything about how it went at Jack's the other day. Do you want to talk about it?"

What was she suppose to say? That there were

lots of people there, that some of them were laughing, that Jack was outside crying? "I don't think I like God anymore."

Her mother stopped peeling. "That's a terrible thing to say, Leona."

"I can't help it. He lets bad things happen. If it were my brother, I'd hate God. I'd never go visit Him at church again. I'd just pretend He was like Santa Claus or something, and wasn't real."

Her mother came over to the counter, looked down at her, gently brushing the hair from her face. "You can't blame God, honey. Wars are started by men, not God."

Just then, the doorbell rang and they both turned at the sound.

"Who could that be on a Sunday morning?" asked her mother.

Leo jumped up. "Maybe it's Cindy." She rushed to the side door and peeked past the curtain. In the driveway was her Grandpa's big, shiny car. She yanked the door open, amazed. "Hi, Grandpa! What are you doing here?"

"Is that the way they've taught you to answer the door?" Her grandfather gave her a stern look, then handed her a quarter.

"Gee, thanks."

"Where's your mother?"

"In the kitchen," Leo replied, turning the coin over in her hand, still wondering why he was there. Even though he lived a lot closer than Memere and Pepere, he had never come to their house, and they rarely went to his. When they did, she always had the feeling that he was waiting for them to leave as soon as they got there. He had the kind of house where she had to wear her Easter clothes just to sit on the furniture, and though the rooms were full of beautiful things, she could never touch them.

"Who is it, Leona?" called her mother.

"Grandpa!" Leo yelled, then she told her grandfather, "Come on, I'll show you where the kitchen is."

Her mother stood stiffly beside one of the red stools, her hands running over her house dress as if it would change her outfit. "I'm sorry. I wasn't expecting company," she managed to say.

"I won't stay. I just wanted to see how you were making out."

"I'm fine. Thank you. We're all fine."

Leo stared at her grandfather. He looked too big for the kitchen. She watched his large hands spin his felt hat, studied the raised line of bushy eyebrows as he asked, "I meant how are you doing financially. You never return my calls."

"We don't need anything. Thank you."

"I just thought you might need a little more help."

Her mother laughed nervously. "I need the kind of help money can't buy."

Leo's grandfather suddenly looked at her as though he'd forgotten she was there. "How do you like your school? I heard your grades are finally improving."

She looked up at him. "That's 'cause there's nothing to do there but study. I hate it, I wish I never had to go back."

At first Leo didn't know what happened. She just felt hot pain on the side of her face where her grandfather's slap had landed.

"You just be grateful for being there. Who do you think's picking up the tab for that education anyway? Not your father."

Her mother pushed past her. "Don't you *ever* hit one of my children again."

Leo, hand over her cheek, leaned against the small of her mother's back. Her mother's body was trembling, but her voice was steady. "You think buying them an education makes up for not having a father? You put him where he is, you and that damn business. You destroyed him years ago. He never had a chance because he had too much heart."

Her grandfather pointed his finger like a gun and aimed it at her mother. "Now you just hold on. I came over here to help out, to make sure you're doing okay. And this is the way you treat me?"

"You came over here to see me humiliated, to rub my nose in the fact that you've been paying the bills. I've never been afraid of you, and that's what it's all about, isn't it?"

"I expected a little common courtesy. I've always taken care of my own."

"You don't own us. You don't own your son or our lives. And I'll see you get paid back every blessed penny, if I have to go to work myself to get it. He never wanted your money. All he ever wanted was your love. Now, please, just leave. Leave me alone before I say anything more."

"You have no right to talk to . . . "

"Don't you yell at my mother!" Leo stepped from behind the safety of her mother's dress, and glared at her grandfather, her fists tight, ready to strike him.

Her grandfather looked down at her, at the angry brown eyes, a replica of his own. Then he put his hat on and strode out of the room.

Leo ran after him, and drawing her hand back, let the quarter fly. "Take that with you!" The coin bounced off the door casing and rolled into the hall, but her grandfather was already down the side steps, moving toward his shiny car.

Her mother dropped into a chair, shaking hands covering her face. "He has everyone in his hip pocket, but damn it, he'll never have me."

"Don't cry, Ma. He's gone."

"I didn't mean to say those things in front of you, Leo."

"I hope I never see him again."

Her mother took Leo's hand and held it in her own. "Don't say that, honey."

"Why not? He hit me, and he made you cry."

"He didn't mean to hit you. He was angry at me. He doesn't know much about children, Leo-- he's from the old school. He loves you in his own way."

Leo touched her cheek. "He sure has a funny way of showing it."

All the way back to the Academy, Leo ran the scene with her grandfather over in her mind. She had only a slight understanding of what the angry words spoken had meant. Though she hadn't known about it, the part about his paying the bills was clear enough. What escaped her was what her mother had meant when she'd said, "You destroyed him years ago."

Leo had never seen her grandfather lose his temper before. It had frightened her, and made her wonder what it must have been like for her father as a kid. It explained why he was quick to hit them--with a father like that, he'd probably gotten worse growing up. And unlike her, he hadn't had a mother to love him. His mother had died when he was Mikey's age, and although she'd often gone with him to put flowers on his mother's grave, she'd never really thought about what it must have been like for him to grow up without her.

The thoughts of his mother turned to thoughts of her own. After her grandfather slapped her, the look in her mother's eyes had even scared Leo. She'd seen a side of her mother she'd never known. A side that wasn't afraid to stand up to a man three times her size. It's just a good thing for him he left when he did, thought Leo; if he'd stayed any longer her mother might have belted him with the potato pot.

The pressure within the walls was building again. There was too much to deal with: Jack's brother, her grandfather, her speech the next day. Hers was one of the three selected from her class and with so much going on, she hadn't even told her mother about it. It was all too much to handle at once, so she stifled the unasked questions, pushed the scenes into a box in a corner of her mind and sealed the lid. Perhaps someday she'd remember it, pry it open, and know the answers.

The next afternoon, Leo sat rigidly in a metal chair, tightly holding her speech as the students, parents, and teachers filled the auditorium at St. Christopher's. She stared down at the papers in her hands, rubbing their edges with nervous fingers. After she'd left Jack's house she'd gone home and rewritten part of her speech. She hadn't told Sister Marie about it; she just figured she'd read it the new way. Now, looking around the room, she was having second thoughts. What if Sister didn't like it? What if. . . Frig her, thought Leo, I don't care if none of them like it.

The program began with the Pledge Of Allegiance, then the principle, Sister Rita, gave a short address. Leo didn't listen; she sat shuffling her papers, rehearsing her speech in her mind.

Olive walked across the stage to the podium and curtsied. Olive was decked out in a pink dress with matching sash and nylons. Leo leaned over and yanked up her knee socks. She felt ugly in her uniform and wondered if what she was wearing would make a difference to the judges.

Olive and Lisa's speeches were over too quickly. Leo had been too nervous to listen to either of them. When Sister Rita finally called her name she felt like running off the stage. Just pretend it's a swim meet she told herself for courage.

The applause for Lisa was over and the auditorium grew quiet. Leo stood up and walked over to the podium, one of her shoes clicking from a loose heel. Standing up on the step stool, she leaned forward, and took hold of the microphone. Without looking down at her paper, she began the speech she knew by heart, concentrating on the words instead of the sea of faces

"Democracy means, 'a government of the people, by the people, for the people.' It means the citizens of the United States have the right to elect their President and politicians. It means they have the right to vote for whoever they feel will do the best job. In a Democratic society, we are all equal and should have equal rights no matter if you are black, or white, or Italian, or a woman, or even a kid."

Some of the adults laughed, and Leo waited until they were finished.

"In America a person can say and write whatever they want because Democracy means freedom. Freedom to live, and think, and work as we want. It gives us the right to practice any religion, and gives us the right to be anything we want. A doctor, a nurse, or even a nun.

"In Russia there is no Democratic society. They believe in a thing called Communism. I am not sure

exactly what that means. I only know they can't say or write what they want. They can't practice religion or be who they want. I am glad I don't live there.

"Sister Marie says we are fighting in Vietnam in order to stop the spread of Communism. She says we are fighting so the people there can have a Democratic society like we have. So they will have freedom like we do."

A stir in the audience caused Leo to hesitate just long enough to catch Sister Marie shake her head at Sister Rita.

"Vietnam is such a tiny place that it took me an hour to find it on the globe in our classroom. I told my friend Jack it was a small place to fight for Democracy.

"I think Democracy is worth fighting for, and I hope we are fighting in Vietnam because of it, like Sister Marie says. That way, Jack's brother Nick, got killed for a reason."

Leo took her papers, and ignoring Sister Marie's wondering stare, went back to her seat. For a long moment the hall was quiet, then people began to clap, and a couple of the parents even stood up. She looked out at them and smiled, knowing it didn't matter what Sister Marie would do to her for changing her speech. She'd said what she'd felt, and it was right.

The trophy's gold plate read: Voice Of Democracy, 1966; First Place--5th Grade. She'd discovered that the pool wasn't the only place where she could win. She'd also gotten her picture in the town's weekly newspaper and had sent a copy home to her mother. A week later, she received a card of congratulations from her grandfather with a ten dollar bill inside. It reminded her of that Sunday morning when he'd showed up out of the blue, and how he'd treated her and her mother. She sent the ten dollars back to him with a note that read:

I don't want your money.
I just want your love.

Your grandkid,

Leo

XII.

FREE AT LAST

"Like Calsa says, 'Man, the shit really hit the fan.'" Leo leaned back against the brick building and waited with Angie for the recess bell. That morning Sister Theresa had discovered her letter stash. Leo had been making her bed when one of the letters had fallen on the floor. It hadn't taken the nun long to find the other five tucked beneath her mattress.

"What'd they say?" Angie asked, her eyes rounding with fear.

"Don't worry, I didn't tell on you. I told them I mailed the letters, and as far as you go, you don't know nothin' about it, right?"

"Right," said Angie, but her face was still creased with worry. "Did they hit you?"

"No, I was surprised. Sister St. Paul just said I couldn't go home the next free weekend. She was mad and hollered and stuff, but she didn't hit me. Gave me the usual stuff about it going on my

Permanent Record, but that's only a big deal to her. The way I look at it, I got so much junk on my *Permanent Record* already, that by the time I get to be Mark's age they'll have to haul it around in Dan Dan The Rubbish Man's dump truck--and who's gonna bother to read all that." Leo smiled. "She did try to bribe me though. She said if I told her the names of the girls, she'd let me go home for that weekend. I told you it was a smart idea not to have them sign their letters or put their return address on the envelopes."

"So did you tell on them?"

"No way. She said I had till Friday to make up my mind, but I told Evette to tell the others I won't fink on them. They trusted us, you know? Besides, Evette would never rat on me anymore than Huck would rat on Jim." Leo let out a big sigh. "Thing is, my mother's birthday's that weekend. I really want to go home."

"You didn't tell them about the money part, did you?" asked Angie.

"Are you crazy?" said Leo, shaking her head. "I told them I did it 'cause we live in a Democratic society and that I was just trying to help. See, I figured if they thought I did it because I wanted to help, like collecting for the pagan babies or something, then they wouldn't be as mad. But if I told them I got paid for it, too, boy! Besides, it ain't right that they read our mail. Evette says it's an invasion of privacy."

"What's that mean?" asked Angie.

Leo hesitated, then told her, "It's like walking

in the bathroom when someone's using it."

Leo wasn't sure why Sister St. Paul had given her until Friday to make up her mind. The way Leo looked at it, there wasn't anything to make up her mind about: she couldn't tell, and that was that. Still, she did have qualms about not going home. Unlike the Mexicans and a dozen of the other girls who lived too far to travel--like Evette, who lived in New York City, or Calsa, who lived in Washington D.C., or Doris who lived way up in Fort Kent--Leo had never stayed at the Academy during a free weekend. Just the thought of having to stay made her want to go home even more. Added to that desire was the guilt and disappointment of having to miss her mother's birthday. And as luck would have it, she and Maggie got a letter from their father saying he was coming home from the hospital for good. It was the news she'd been waiting to hear since he'd left at Christmas, and the thought of not getting to see him until Easter was almost more than she could bear.

With a clear conscious, but a heavy heart, she entered Sister St. Paul's office on Friday afternoon.

Sister St. Paul was sitting at her desk. "So?" she asked, her eyebrows lifting with the word. "Did you make up your mind to do the right thing?"

In Leo's mind not telling on her friends was the right thing, and she automatically nodded.

190

Misinterpreting Leo's response, a smile of victory spread across the nun's face. "I'm glad your father's more important than your stubbornness, Leona. I'm also glad he's getting out of the hospital."

"Who told you about that?" Then it hit her-- Sister had read hers and Maggie's letter. It was like a punch in the stomach--a reminder of how and why she'd gotten into this mess in the first place.

"It doesn't matter who told me," said Sister, reaching for a piece of paper.

It matters to me, thought Leo. "If my father wanted you to read his letter he would have put your name on it."

"Your parents are fully aware of the school policies, Leona. So stop trying to change the subject." The nun picked up her pen. "Now what are the names? I don't have time to play games with you."

Leo gave her a confused look. "I didn't come in here to tell you that, Sister. I came in here to do the right thing."

The nun closed her eyes, and shook her head slowly. "I'm loosing my patience, Leona."

Leo studied the floor and nervously raked at a hang nail. She just wanted to get this over with; get out of this room that felt like a shoe box, and smelled like a hot radiator. When she looked back up, Sister's foxy-eyes were peering at her.

"You know this means you won't be able to go home," the nun threatened.

"Yes, Sister."

"Your father will be very disappointed, Leona.

You know that, don't you?"

Leo rubbed her tongue over her chipped tooth. "Yes, Sister. But I think if he knew I had to fink on my friends to go home, he'd probably want me to stay here."

Sister St. Paul sighed and tried another approach. "Of course this means I'll have to write to your mother and explain to her why you won't be home that weekend."

Leo bit down on her lip, holding back what was burning to come out--why don't you tell her what you did to my hat while you're at it! You never wrote home about that!

"I'll have to tell her that you consider your friends more important than your family."

Leo winced. "That's not true."

"I know she will be very upset about it," Sister continued. "If this was not such a serious matter, I would relent only because of her. God has given her a difficult test this past year. It seems he has given me one, too."

"Can I go now, Sister?"

"Yes, you may go. But before you do, I just want to let you know that I already know the girls who are involved."

Leo stared at her in disbelief. "What?"

"Tell me, Leona, how many girls here are from New York City? And didn't you ever consider that I might recognize the handwriting, or the stationary?"

"Then why . . . "

"Because I wanted to hear it from you. Because I wanted to give you the opportunity to face up to your responsibly and admit that what you did was terribly wrong. That's why."

She tricked me, thought Leo. She made me believe she didn't know; she made me chose between my family and friends, then used them against me. Used them to try and make me say what she wanted to hear, what she already knew. "Maybe some of what I did was wrong," said Leo, referring to the money she'd made mailing the letters. "But what you did, Sister, was a sin."

"Shut the door on your way out, Leona. And I will forget you said that last remark."

"I don't want you to," said Leo, heading for the door. "And you can put that on my *Permanent Record.*"

That evening, the main course in the cafeteria was the conversation that had taken place in Sister St. Paul's office.

" . . . then she told St. Paul that if her father wanted Sister to read his letter he would have put her name on it."

"And that's not all--she said her father would rather have her stay here than squeal on her friends."

"I heard she told Sister St. Paul she'd better go to confession because what Sister had done was a mortal sin."

At first, Leo was surprised to hear slices of her conversation with the nun being passed from table to table, as she hadn't told anyone about what had happened or what had been said.   Ironically, the source of information was Doris, who had an appointment with the nun, and had heard everything as she'd waited by the open door in the hall.   Go figure, thought Leo, and here everyone thought Doris was Sister St. Paul's pet.

Leo's surprise was followed by a feeling of relief. All week, Evette and the others involved in the mailing scheme, had kept her at a distance, afraid she would tell on them in order to go home. Now, despite the fact they'd all been caught, they were throwing her smiles and high-fives from across the room.

Sister St. Paul's trick had backfired--everyone knew the truth, or parts of it: Leo hadn't given in, hadn't told on her friends. Instead, she had, as Calsa put it, "kicked some butt in St. Paul's office."

The Friday of free weekend started off bad and got worse. That morning Leo had collected the trash on all three floors and was about to descend the stairs to the basement when the box split wide open. Gooey shampoo bottles, wads of used Kleenex, balls of hair that looked like Calsa's, and crumpled paper went down the steps in a landslide. By the time she got a new box and cleaned it all up, she was half an hour late for class. To make matters worse, Sister Marie wasn't impressed with her excuse and told her she'd have to make up the time after school.

At three o'clock Leo watched the kids in her class rush for their coats, hooting and hollering with the freedom of a Friday afternoon. It wasn't fair, she thought; it wasn't her fault that she was late. She couldn't let Sister Alphonse clean that up all by herself. It just wasn't fair.

"See you on Monday," Angie told her, then leaned over and whispered, "Maybe she'll let you out early. Do you want me to wait?"

"It's Friday," said Leo. "Get out of here. I would."

"If you say so."

Leo watched her leave, then looked up at Sister Marie coming toward her with a blue rag in her hand. "Leona, I'll be right back. Please take this and dust my desk while I'm gone."

"Yes, Sister."

Knowing Sister's kitty-cat glasses were following her, she walked over to the desk at a slug's pace and pretended to dust, but as soon as she heard the nun step out of the room, she sprinted to the window. From there, she watched the procession of cars drive up to the Academy, watched the girls hug parents, load their suitcases, slam car doors, and wave good-byes. Now she knew how the Mexicans felt--they never got to go home.

The previous night their mother had called to say that Maggie couldn't go home either. She didn't want Leo to spend the weekend by herself. The last thing Maggie had said to her was, "Never talk to me again, brat. It's all your fault I have to stay here."

The weight of that guilt had dragged Leo down all day, had left her feeling tired and defeated. Watching the other girls leave made the loneliness more acute, made her feel powerless, and for a brief second she thought of Hope. Maybe this is how she felt the night she'd done it--like she didn't have a friend in the world.

"What are you doing?"

Leo jumped back from the window. "Nothing, Sister. Just looking."

Sister Marie walked briskly up to her desk and inspected it with her finger. "Leona. You haven't even dusted this." Sister held up her fingers, the evidence coating each tip. "Please do it again, and do it right."

"Yes, Sister."

Leo trudged over to the desk and ran the rag over it, wondering if her father was already home, wondering how her mother was going to feel without them there for her birthday. Inside, the walls began to rumble with injustice--it wasn't fair that Sister St. Paul was punishing her for doing something that was right. What was written in her parents' letters was no one's business but her's and Maggie's. All those private things their father had told them--how he was sorry, how he was going to try and make it up to them--wasn't for that nun to know.

Rage began to push aside her weariness. She and Maggie would be heading home right now if it wasn't for that nun. She hated her, hated this place, hated having to dust this desk when it wasn't her fault the stupid box blew apart.

Sister Marie leaned over the desk, testing for dust, and Leo looked up just in time to see the nun rub the grit between her fingers.

"What's this?" Sister asked, in an accusing tone, then she lifted the desk mat, exposing a perfect line. "And look here!"

Clenching the rag in a tight fist, Leo yelled, "If you can do a better job, do it yourself!" Then she threw the blue wad at the nun.

Sister took a step backward, as if the weight of the rag had thrown her off balance, but quickly recovered and, with an open hand, slapped Leo soundly across the face.

Leo struck back.

Her fist reeled into the nun's stomach with so much force that Sister's cross lifted off her chest. The nun bent over, and Leo dodged her weak attempt to grab her arm. Then she ran toward the door, ripping her coat off its peg on the way.

"Leona! Get back here!"

"Go to hell!"

Tears chilled her face as Leo raced down Main Street. She wanted her mother. She wanted to be home where it was safe, where she could sit in the darkness of her closet and be little again. She stepped off the curb and put her thumb out. Her father was always picking up hitchhikers--someone would stop; someone would give her a ride home.

As she walked backwards along the street, her thumb flagging each passing car, she began to sing Evette's song, the words calming her, giving her courage. "Free at last. Free at last. Thank God

Almighty, we are free at last."

It was the first time she'd sung those words and known what they meant. She thought of the picture in Evette's locker, the picture of the man she called Martin Luther King. Evette had told her it was his favorite song, that he'd used it in a speech, and as Leo continued to sing the refrain, she wondered if it was his favorite because he knew what the words meant, too.

She'd only made it as far as Fred's Hardware when she spotted the flashing blue light. She darted between two parked cars and collided with a pair of legs coming out of the store.

"Whoa there, where you going in such a hurry?" said the man who belonged to the legs.

The officer in the police car jumped out. "Stop that little girl!"

The man she'd run into came toward her. Her head jerked left, then right as she tried to decide which way to run. Finally, she bolted for the alley, almost tripping over a garbage can, sending its lid clamoring across the concrete. She caught herself and jumped forward, clearing the lid, and sped down the narrow tunnel and around the back of Fred's Hardware--right into a blue uniform.

"Got you!" said a deep voice.

She struggled to free herself, hitting with her fists, kicking, saying every bad word she knew. Then she felt the grip loosen and she broke free.

"She bit me!"

Leo sprinted, pumping her arms to make her go faster, but the officer she'd bitten was gaining. A blue arm came across her shoulder. A big hand grabbed her coat. She lost her momentum and fell down hard.

A sharp pain shot up her leg, and throbbed under her fingertips as she grasped her knee. She rolled over just enough to see the cut. It wasn't too deep, but the blood welled up like a puddle.

The hand grabbed her arm and yanked her up. "Come on! I got more important things to do than chase Convent girls." The officer had her by the back of the neck. He shook her, then pointed her in the direction of the alley.

"I hurt my knee! Let go of my neck!" Leo demanded.

The officer let go after securing a grip on her hood. Leo bent down and squeezed her knee, then mopped the blood off with her hands.

"Let's go!"

He tugged on her hood and she stood up, and as he pushed her through the alley, she wiped her bloody hands all over her face. When they neared the entrance to the street, where a small crowd had gathered, she began to struggle. "No!" she hollered. "You can't take me back there! I'll get my lawyers after you!"

Despite her flying fists, the officer managed to drag her out to the sidewalk.

"Is she all right?" asked a woman holding a bag of groceries.

"What's going on here!" bellowed a bearded man. "Leave that little kid alone! Can't you see she's hurt?"

The rest of the crowd joined in.

"Poor thing, can't be more than eight years old. What'd she do, rob a bank?"

"I'm surprised he didn't put cuffs on her!"

The red-faced policeman loosened his grip and Leo looked around at the sympathetic faces.

Sister St. Paul's voice shook as she pointed at the car door. "Get in, Leona."

Leo glared at her, the blood on her face beginning to itch. "I'm not going back there and you can't make me." Then she turned and looked at the crowd. "They won't let me go home. All I want to do is see my mother. It's her birthday."

"Look at those big brown eyes, Willie, don't it break your heart?"

"Must be from the Academy--didn't think they took'em that young."

"Always said those nuns were too hard on them, and I'm Catholic."

"Now, Leona. In the car," Sister St. Paul repeated.

The sentiments of the crowd had given Leo renewed courage. "No!" she shouted defiantly.

Sister St. Paul nodded at the policeman. He picked Leo up from behind and, in spite of her kicking legs and thrashing arms, deposited her into the back seat of the patrol car.

Sister St. Paul slid in beside her and the officer slammed the door. "Okay, folks, show's over," he told the people. "Everyone move on."

"You'd best never touch my kids like that!"

"Ma'am, I said it's over, now go home."

200

"Big man, ain't he Jim, mauling a little girl like that? Where's the Mayor when you need him?"

The officer quickly got into the car and shut his door. "We'd better get out of here while we can, Sister. These folks want more blood. Mine."

Leo stared straight ahead with her arms crossed. The car pulled out, and the officer decided to take the back way rather than drive past the crowd again. He looked in his rear view as they approached the Academy's driveway and told the nun, "I'm sorry, Sister. I didn't hit her. She fell."

Sister St. Paul, who had been silently working on her rosary beads, leaned forward. "I never suspected you did, Officer. Leona is a difficult child. I don't hold you responsible for anything that happened."

The car stopped and Sister opened the door. "Thank you for your help. I assure you this will never happen again."

"I just wish it hadn't turned out like it did. I hope the little kid's okay, Sister."

"She'll be just fine."

"There will probably be some calls put in to the chief. I . . . "

"I'll call him personally and tell him you took what action was necessary. As for the townspeople-- they'll talk for a lack of anything better to do, then forget all about it. "

"Thank you, Sister."

"Come, Leona. I think you've created enough trouble for one day."

Resigned, Leo inched her way across the seat. She looked up at Sister waiting on the stairs, and before getting out of the cruiser, whispered, "Don't worry, she won't beat me too bad."

The officer sighed and Leo heard him say, "I'm never having kids."

As Leo and Sister St. Paul entered the school, Maggie ran to meet them. There was a wild look in her eyes, and Leo watched with amazement as Maggie grabbed the nun's arm and demanded, "What did you do to my sister?"

Sister St. Paul shook her arm free. "Don't you *ever* speak to me in that tone again, young lady. And don't you *ever* touch me."

As if surprised by her own bold actions or expecting the nun to hit her, Maggie reeled backward.

"It's all right, Maggie," Leo told her. "I just fell down."

Sister pushed past Maggie, telling her, "I've had enough of your family for one day, Margaret. Now take your sister up to the infirmary. And when Sister Martha's finished, Leona is to go directly to the dorm. There will be no dinner for her tonight." Sister turned on her heel and shot them a deadly look. "Is that clear?"

"Perfectly," Maggie replied caustically. Then she put her arm around Leo and led her away. "Don't worry, Leo, I'll sneak you something to eat later. Had enough of our family has she? Wait until Ma finds out."

That evening, Leo lay in the dark dorm listening to the girls below play records. The floor vibrated with their dancing and laughter, and she wondered if Maggie was dancing, too. Maggie had stayed with her while Sister Martha put a butterfly stitch on her knee. She had held her hand until all the blood was washed away and the white bandage was in place. Then she'd taken her to the dorm, and, covering her with a blanket, promised she would stay. But Leo didn't want Maggie to get in trouble. After all, Maggie would be home if it weren't for her. She'd finally convinced her sister to go, pointing out that if Maggie stayed, she wouldn't be able to sneak any food.

Being in the dorm in the dark by herself was kind of scary. She kept looking over at Hope's alcove, certain that the curtain moved when she looked at it from the corner of her eye. Although there was a waiting list for girls who wanted an alcove, no one had asked to move into Hope's. Leo was glad. It meant the other girls hadn't forgotten Hope, despite the fact that Leo's sign in the chapel had disappeared.

The hiss and clank of the radiator echoed through the empty dorm, and to Leo it almost sounded like voices. "Leona's a difficult child!" "Your father will be very disappointed!" "I'll have to write to your mother!" "What you did was terribly wrong!"

To drown them out, she buried her face into the damp pillow and, clutching her charged visor, told herself over and over, "I ain't bad, I ain't bad," until she fell into exhausted sleep.

"Yesterday was the last straw."

Leo sat in a chair in the office looking blankly out the window while Sister St. Paul paced the room.

"Your performance in front of the townspeople did nothing for our reputation. What they must have thought!"

A paper-thin smile touched Leo's lips as she remembered the sympathetic faces.

"Your whole problem is your attitude . . ."

There's that word again, thought Leo.

". . . You have no respect for authority. No fear of reprisal . . ."

Grownups always brought up attitude when they were mad at her. She used to get it mixed up with altitude until Mabel set her straight. She'd told Mabel she couldn't bake a cake unless her attitude was right.

". . .That makes you dangerous, Leona. Because you don't care." Sister's eyes hardened with anger. "Do you have any idea how humiliated I was? All those people looking at me like that? Like I was some kind of a . . ." Sister halted, stood stiffly with her back to Leo. "Yesterday was the last straw," she repeated. "Putting on that show, hitting Sister Marie, telling her to . . ."

Leo looked up, wondering it the nun would say *go to hell*, and was disappointed when she didn't.

"I just can't have it." Sister walked over to the desk and sat down. "I called your mother."

Surprise, surprise, thought Leo--but I bet you didn't mention Hope while you were on the phone. It never happened, did it? No one tries to kill themselves in your school.

"I told her we wouldn't accept you back in the fall."

Leo suddenly straightened in her chair.

"I told her you could finish out the year. . ."

Next year she didn't have to come back?

". . . There are only two months left, and I have put up with you this long."

There is a God, thought Leo, and I'll never blame Him for anything again.

"It was no easy task, breaking the news to her. She was Valedictorian when she graduated from here, and your grandmother, too. You are the first, in three generations . . .You've broken a tradition. Do you have any idea what that means?"

For the first time since she'd entered the room, Leo spoke. "It means I don't have to come back here next year." A big smile stretched across her face.

Sister sighed and lifted her hands in a gesture of defeat, her palms facing the ceiling. "Leave, Leona. There is nothing more I want to say to you. I can not reach you and I am done trying."

"Thank you, Sister," she said, and meant it.

As she jumped and skipped down the corridor outside the office, Leo sang at the top of her lungs. "Free at last. Free at last. Thank God Almighty, I'm free at last!

XIII.

Broken Houses

Any fears Leo had about her mother's reaction to Sister St. Paul's decision and the event that had prompted that decision were put to rest a few days later. As usual, the baby-blue envelope was already opened when Leo received it, and for the third time during afternoon study hall, she reread her mother's letter.

> *Dear Leo,*
>
> *Your father and I were both terribly upset to hear what happened. Having talked with Maggie on the phone this evening, I have a better understanding of what went on. I was relieved to hear that your knee wasn't hurt too badly. As Maggie probably told you by now, I wanted to talk with you myself, but you were sleeping when I called and I thought it best not to wake you. Still, it troubled me to think of you having to stay in the*

dorm by yourself after being injured in a fall, and that you hadn't been given anything for supper. I was glad I hadn't allowed Maggie to come home, and that she was there to comfort you as best as she could. I will call you again in a few days to see how you are doing.

Both Dad and I agree with Sister St. Paul about your not returning in the fall. However, we think it best if you finish out the year. There is not much time remaining and you have done so well with your grades. Whether Maggie returns to St. Mary's next year, will be a decision I will leave up to her. According to Maggie, Sister St. Paul "has had enough of our family."

I want you to know, Leo, that we understand why you tried to run away. We know you miss us, as we miss you, but running away, as I'm sure you have learned, was a dangerous thing to do. If you feel you can not finish out the year, just call me, and we will come and get you. But PLEASE, promise me you will not try to run away again.

It has been a rough year for all of us, and I know it has been especially hard on you being away from home. Just know we are not angry at you in any way, and that we love you. God bless you and keep you strong. Remember to say your prayers, and as always, listen to the voice that tells you what is right.

> Love,
> Mom, Dad, and Brothers

Leo carefully folded the letter and returned it to

its envelope. She was lucky to have a mother like she had--how many other mothers would still love their kid after they'd been kicked out of so many schools. Although her mother said they weren't angry at her, and understood why she'd tried to run away, she still felt guilty for the trouble and worry she'd caused her parents. She promised herself she'd stick out the rest of the year no matter what it took. Besides, just knowing she didn't have to sleep another night in this place if she didn't want to, made it easier to stay.

After tucking the letter between the pages of her math book, she looked over at Maggie. How had their mother put it--according to Maggie, Sister St. Paul "has had enough of our family." I wish I could have seen Sister's face when she read that, thought Leo, then she covered her mouth with her hand, and bit into her palm to control the bubbling laughter.

"Leona, no laughing during study hall," said Sister Bernedette, who was monitoring the room.

"Sorry, Sister Bernedette," Leo giggled. "I was just having a funny thought."

"Well, keep it to yourself, dear, people are trying to study."

"Yes, Sister."

On Good Friday, Memere came to pick up the Leo and Maggie for Easter vacation. Before they'd left the school, Memere and Sister St. Paul had had a talk. Leo wasn't sure what it was about, as both of them had spoken in French. But Memere's French had sounded sharp and her hands were flying more than usual as she spoke. If Pepere were there, Leo knew he would have said, "Memere's got a bee in her bonnet."

But now that they were on the road, Memere was her happy self again and eager to tell them what was happening on the farm--Pepere was done tapping the hard maples; the syrup had been boiled down and bottled; the mallards had come back to the pond.

It felt good to be moving, to feel the breeze from the window pushing against her face. It had been a tiring afternoon: during the three hours of silence that honor Christ's death, they had attended the Stations of the Cross. Father Richie had done the long version, and by the time they'd gotten to the fourteenth cross, even the nuns were yawning.

"And you know your Pepere," said her grandmother, "he has to have his peas by the Fourth of July. He's worse than a dog with a bad case of fleas; just itching to get in his garden."

As Leo listened to Memere's warm chatter, she watched out the window, each passing telephone pole bringing her closer to home. The grass was not yet green, the ground still soft with mud, but spring was here and like Pepere, she was itching, too: itching to play baseball, to fly a kite down in Douglas Field, to dig a hole and play marbles. Itching to get home.

A half hour later, she was running up the front

walk, yelling, "Ma! Ma! We're home!"

The door opened before Leo even made it up the steps. "I'm right here, honey," laughed her mother.

Leo threw her arms around her mother's waist and buried her face into the soft fabric of her cotton dress. I'm here, she thought, I'm here.

"Boy did I miss you," said her mother, stroking Leo's back.

Leo held on, wanting the moment to last forever. "I missed you, too. I thought Easter would never come." Leo peeked up at her mother. "And Maggie wants to go back there next year--can you believe it?"

Her mother's hand caressed Leo's hair. "When I was her age, I loved that school, too. It was a safe place to be with the war on."

"It ain't the same, Ma; and there's a war going on now, too."

Her mother shifted her weight and gave a nostalgic sigh. "I'd even thought of entering the convent then. Now look at me. Five children and a husband who . . ."

"Who what, Ma?"

"Oh, don't listen to me, sweetie, I was just thinking out loud." Her mother gave her a tight hug. "It's so good to have you home."

Her mother let go of her to welcome Maggie and Memere, and Leo glanced around at the holiday touches--the white lilies, their pots dressed in pink and yellow foil; the line of baskets waiting to be filled by two legged bunnies; the Little King, dressed in purple robes.

Leo drifted over to the Easter baskets, and ran a finger over one of the colored handles. She'd given up candy for Lent and just the thought of that basket being filled with chocolate eggs and jelly beans was torture. "Next year I'm giving up lima beans for Lent," she declared.

"But you hate lima beans," said Hal, who had just come down the stairs and was heading toward her for a hug.

Leo felt her brother's strong arms tighten around her. "Yeah," she agreed. "Just think how easy it'll be."

Two days after Easter, Leo sat alone in the den, chewing the last of her jelly beans and thinking how things had changed since Christmas. The politeness had worn off now that her father was home for good. Mark, used to running the house while their father was gone, seemed angry at him for being back. And her father seemed angry at Mark for taking his place while he was gone. She'd noticed Mikey seemed confused, too. He'd gotten used to Mark being the one who took him to Cub Scouts, or church, or to birthday parties; he'd also gotten used to Mark telling him what he could or couldn't do. Now that their father was back, Mikey wasn't sure who he was supposed to listen to, or who was supposed to take him places. It put him in a bad spot: no matter which one he turned to, the other got hurt. Leo knew the whole thing weighed heavily on her little brother's mind because he'd started stuttering again.

She'd also noticed that Hal was never around. He breezed in and out like the wind. Or as Maggie put it, "He's only here long enough to change his clothes and fill his face." The night before he'd come home at two in the morning with a black eye and a big story, and didn't seem to care if anyone believed him or not.

But since she and Maggie had come home for vacation, there hadn't been any fights. Despite their anger or hurt feelings, Mark and her father seemed to have a truce going, and they were both doing their best to make it all work. So was she.

A noise in the hall interrupted her thoughts. At first she thought it was Mabel getting her coat to leave for the day. But when Mabel didn't call good-bye, she jumped off the couch and went out to investigate.

Her father was standing next to the antique chest. He still had his coat on, and didn't seem to hear her. She watched as he raised his arm. Then she saw the familiar bottle with its clear liquid and its scary bird label: Vodka.

She took a step forward, asking in a shaky voice, "What are you doing, Dad?"

Her father didn't turn around. "I'm just checking."

"Checking what?" she whispered.

Her father faced her. "I keep this here, just in case. See, it hasn't even been opened." He held it up for her to look at.

"In case of what?"

He put the bottle back in the top drawer.

"In case of what, Dad?"

He spun around and growled, "In case I need it."

She flinched at his tone.

Her father sat down on the hard chair that no one ever used. "I didn't mean to yell at you, Leo. I'm sorry."

Leo didn't move. The jelly beans in her left hand began to melt and she looked down at the colors dying her fingers.

"It's just . . . it's hard. I'm trying. I don't know what to tell you . . . you're too young to understand."

I'm old enough to know you love that bottle more than me, thought Leo.

"Don't look at me that way, Leo. I told you I was sorry. I didn't mean to yell at you . . . Please don't tell your mother."

She began to shake from the effort of holding back the anger. "Don't you think she knows?" she asked, but didn't wait for an answer.

Leo made her way down Elizabeth Road, hands deep in her pockets. Since she'd been home he'd been sober and everything was great--no fights, no name calling, no reactions. Now he was going to wreck it. How could he do that to them?

If he started drinking again, they'd probably ship her off for good, probably send her to some school in China or Russia. She walked up the front steps, pushed the doorbell and waited. When no one answered, she pushed again, noticing that the Christmas wreath was still on the door. It was dried up, and rust colored, the ribbon faded, water stained.

The door opened a crack, then wider.

"Hello, Leo." Jack's mother stood in the doorway, clutching her bathrobe.

"Is Jack home?"

"Jack isn't here."

"When will he be back?"

"Back? I'm not sure. Soon, I think."

Leo took in the uncombed hair, the pale face, the wrinkled robe. "Could I come back later?" she asked. "It's kinda important."

"Certainly. He'll be home soon. I'm sure of it." She started to close the door, but an arm reached out and opened it wider.

"Hi, Leo," said Jack. "Come on in."

"I'm sorry." His mother stepped aside so Leo could enter. "I didn't know you were home."

"That's okay, Mom. I was down cellar."

"Have you been home long? I didn't hear you come in."

"You were sleeping. I didn't want to bother you."

"Oh." His mother smiled at Leo. "He's so thoughtful. Just like his brother."

"We'll be down cellar, Mom." Jack took Leo's arm and led her through the living room and kitchen. "Don't mind the mess," he told her, opening the cellar door. "I didn't have time to pick up today."

Leo looked at the dirty dishes littering the table,

the counter, piled up in the sink. "That's okay," she told him. "Our place looks like this all the time, and we've got Mabel."

She followed Jack to the basement. She'd never been down there before: gray concrete walls, a washer, dryer, a work bench, an old stuffed chair. Her cellar was all pine paneled with a tiled floor. She shivered and zipped up her coat.

"You cold?" Jack asked, picking up a hand full of darts.

"No, I'm fine."

Jack aimed a dart and fired at the board. "So how's that school of yours? Get kicked out yet?"

"Yup. They ain't letting me come back next year 'cause I got in too much trouble. I even ran away, but I didn't get too far."

Jack laughed, threw another dart. "I'm surprised you lasted this long. Where will you go next year? There aren't any Catholic schools left, are there?"

"Who cares. I hope they send me to public school."

Jack looked over at her. "What's the matter?"

Leo flopped into the stuffed chair. "My father got out of the hospital," she said, then started picking at the chair's worn fabric.

"You don't look too happy about it."

"I'm not. That's why I'm here."

"What happened?"

"I caught him in the hall with a bottle. It wasn't open but he's not supposed to have any in the house. He'll do it again. I know it. He'll spoil everything."

"I remember how you used to call him The Old

215

Man. I used to think that was funny." Jack smiled at her, but Leo turned away. "Come on, Leo, maybe he just keeps it around. My father keeps a pack of cigarettes on the shelf in the kitchen and he hasn't smoked in ten years."

"He told me not to tell my mother."

Jack retrieved the darts, positioned himself behind the line of tape. "Will you?" he asked.

"No," she told him. "I don't want to be the one who wrecks it for her . . . She probably knows, anyway. I hate him, no kidding. I wish he never came home from the hospital."

Jack looked over at her, catching her gaze, holding it. "You don't hate him, Leo. You just hate what he does."

"What's the difference, Jack?"

"You don't hate him; he's your father. What you hate is that he drinks."

Leo leaned back in the musty smelling chair. She'd never thought of it like that before. A noise overhead made her look up at the ceiling, and staring at the pipes, she asked, "Is your mother sick, Jack?"

Jack threw a dart with more force and it ricocheted off the metal rim. "You could say that. She's going to a doctor."

"What's she got?"

"The doctor says its depression." Jack paused, as though looking for another way to say it. "She hasn't been right since my brother . . ."

"Oh," Leo said, understanding.

"She's got a shrine for him upstairs: all his pictures. I loved him too, you know, but . . . She doesn't even get dressed anymore, just sleeps all day or watches those friggin' home movies of us as kids." Jack jabbed the darts into the board, then walked over and sat on the arm of Leo's chair.

Leo moved over slightly to give him more room. "Will she get better?"

"I don't know. My father never tells me anything. He just goes to church a lot. Like it will help. I quit going."

"Not even on Sundays?"

Jack shook his head.

"Ain't you afraid of going to hell?"

Jack stretched his arms out behind his head. "Can't be worse than living here. They're always fighting now. See, she blames my father. But it wasn't his fault Nick didn't want to go to college. She's always after him about it--if I hear that friggin' college thing one more time . . ."

"I guess I'm not the only one with a broke house."

Jack reached over, brushed Leo's bangs out of her eyes. "I miss your hat."

The feel of his fingers felt nice against her face, felt like her mother's touch. "So do I. I'm still trying to forgive them. I made a deal with God about it." She looked away, her eyes growing misty with the memory of Old Orchard. "Why does he do it, Jack?"

"I don't know, Leo," Jack answered softly. "Maybe he needs it. Like she needs that shrine up there."

She turned and looked at him, saw the hurt in

his eyes, a reflection of her own. He knew how she felt. "Thanks, Jack."

He reached over and gave her shoulder a squeeze. "Hey, what are friends for."

Leo sniffed and rubbed her eyes with the back of her hand. "So," she said. "You think the Dodgers will win the World Series again?"

Jack laughed. "With Sandy Koufax pitching?"

"Ain't he great," Leo agreed. "First guy ever to pitch a perfect game."

As the conversation turned away from Jack's mother and her father, the basement didn't seem so cold. And as they debated Koufax's chances of breaking his record of four no-hitters, and yakked about things like the Russian astronaut that had floated in space, and what they would do next summer, they left their broken houses behind, and, for a while, all seemed right in the world.

XIV.

LEO WAS HERE!

T he lilacs were flowering; it was light until seven-thirty; the last semester of school was almost over; and Leo stood in the corridor, humming and looking up at the red bell. The bell: the heartbeat of the school, the ruler of their lives, had met its match. She already had a screwdriver hidden in her locker, but the ladder she needed was in the gym. The older girls had been using it all week to put up decorations for their prom.

"Hey, Leo, get the door!"

Through the window in the side door she saw Stella and Doris carrying Sister Alphonse's ladder up the steps. She held the door for them, laughing as she watched them wrestle with the ladder, maneuvering it through the entrance like Laurel and Hardy. After resting it against the wall, the two girls collapsed to the floor.

"Phew!" said Stella, shaking her arms out.

"What are you talking about?" panted Doris.

"I'm the one who carried most of it."

"If they want it in the basement," Stella continued, "they can come and get it."

Doris sighed in agreement. "I'm not carrying it one more foot. Not one more inch."

Leo couldn't believe it. Here was the ladder not five feet from the bell. It was as if God wanted her to do it.

"I don't know how you talked me into this," Calsa whispered.

"Shh! And hold the light better," Leo told her. "I keep losing the screw hole."

"My feet are freezing. I don't see why we had to come barefoot."

"I told you. Slippers make too much noise; you can hear them a mile away." Holding her breath, Leo turned the screwdriver's handle with all her might, and the screw turned another notch. "This is the longest damn screw in the whole world," she said, then dropped her arms to give them a rest.

"You just took a break," Calsa whispered sharply. "The way you're going, we'll still be here at breakfast."

Leo buried her face in her hands and snorted with laughter.

Calsa, whose busy hair was wilder than usual, tilted her head backward, her hair sticking straight out like Bozo the clown. "What's so funny now?"

she demanded. "Really, if you have one more laugh attack, I'm going back to bed."

Calsa's threat sobered Leo enough so she could talk. "They won't know it's time for breakfast 'cause the bell ain't gonna ring."

Calsa's cackle boomeranged off the walls and Leo hurriedly resumed her task. Cripe, they probably heard her all the way to Portland, thought Leo, as she gave the screw another twist. Then she felt something pop loose and the bell's metal clapper went flying.

"Ow, something just hit me in the head."

"It was the dinger," Leo told her. "We need it back. Check your hair, it's probably stuck in it."

"I'll stuck you," Calsa mumbled.

Leo looked down from her perch. In the dark, Calsa looked like a big, black bear crawling around on the floor.

"Got it," said Calsa.

"Good. Give it to me. I've got to screw it on just a little so it's upside-down. That way they'll think it just came loose."

"Won't it still hit the bell?" Calsa asked, pointing the flashlight into Leo's eyes.

"You trying to blind me? Give me that dinger."

"Ding, ding, ding." Calsa laughed, then doubled over. "God, I think I peed my pants."

"Give me it to me now, and wet your pants later," said Leo, holding out her hand.

Calsa reached up and thrust the piece of metal into Leo's waiting palm. "No shit, I think I peed myself."

Leo re-fastened the clapper upside-down and carefully tightened it just enough to hold its metal arm in place. "No way it's gonna ring now."

"No bells tomorrow, thanks to us," giggled Calsa.

"Not thanks to us," Leo told her. "Thanks to God."

The next morning without the bell to wake them, even the nuns in the Mother House overslept. Mass had to be canceled. Breakfast was late being served, its menu changed to toast and cold cereal.

Over their empty bowls, the girls lingered in the clock-less cafeteria, laughing and waiting for the chore bell that was never going to ring. When Sister St. Paul finally arrived with a fistful of whistles, she announced, "I know this will disappoint all of you, but if school is to be started on time, chores must be canceled for today."

The room erupted in a rowdy applause; girls drummed their silverware against the tables; some yiped like happy dogs; and most remarkable of all, Sister St. Paul didn't try to stop it--she was laughing too. For a joyous minute, it was if the teachers and their leader were as young and crazy as the girls.

Leo was impressed with the chaos--it far exceeded her imagined expectations. It amazed her how one red bell with an automatic timer had so much power. How its silence could cause so much freedom and laughter. And knowing she was partly responsible for all those smiles almost made her want to take the credit. Instead, she looked over at Calsa and mouthed "Thank God."

All day the nuns ran around blowing whistles and screeching the time. The girls took advantage of the situation and pleasure in their good excuses: "Sorry I'm late, Sister, I never heard the bell." "But I don't have a watch Sister, I didn't know free time was over." "The bell never rang, Sister, and we couldn't hear your whistle outside."

In the rec hall after supper that evening the two culprits huddled in a corner.

"Sister Rita thought it was a short in the office timer," whispered Calsa. "She played with that most of the day."

"I didn't think it would take her this long," Leo giggled. "She's good about fixin' things. Ever see her tool box? She's got so many screwdrivers she hasn't even missed the one I borrowed."

"I heard tomorrow St. Paul's calling in an electrician if Sister Rita can't fix it."

"We don't have to worry about that," Leo reassured her. "Sister St. Paul said the same thing about the incinerator when that broke down. Remember?"

"Yeah," said Calsa. "Sister Rita made Sister Theresa stand outside in the dark with a flashlight till she got it running again."

"No doubt about it," said Leo. "Sister Fixit won't go to bed till she figures it out, and tomorrow she'll get to be St. Paul's hero again while I'm collectin' two days of trash."

Leo's assumption was correct. Sister Rita, the mechanical whiz of the convent, finally found and easily fixed the problem. But for one glorious day the heart of the school had stopped beating, and Sister Rita's technical explanation as to why, was only fully understood by Calsa and Leo.

Prom day finally arrived and excited voices filled the halls as Leo trudged along collecting trash. She passed by the demerit board where Calsa was tallying up her marks. They looked at each other and burst out laughing. "Better check your pants," Leo told her, then continued down the hall.

"Watch where you're going, Leona!" cried Sister St. Paul, after dodging the cardboard box. "You're always running me over with that thing."

"Sorry, Sister, I must have been lost in thought."

"Well, just be careful and stay out of my way; there's too much to do. I need to get the flowers and check on the food. And I want this place ship-shape in all quarters."

Leo watched the nun march off, then saluted her. "Aye, aye, Sister. Ship-shape in all quarters!"

The nun spun on her heel, her shoes clicking sharply. "Don't be fresh, Leona. I don't have time today."

Leo smiled at her. "Just kidding you, Sister."

The nun tapped her foot with indecision, then

barked at Calsa instead. "Don't worry, Calsa, you still have the demerit record."

Leo watched the nun hurry off. Sister St. Paul let her get away with a lot more stuff now, and she figured it was because she wasn't coming back in the fall and the nun didn't want to waste any time on her. Still, if Sister had found out about the bell, thought Leo, she would have found some time to waste in a hurry. The funny thing was, now that Sister St. Paul had given up on her, and was done "trying to reach her," they'd almost become friends. Sister no longer hassled her about pulling up her socks, no longer kept a constant watch. The short leash had become a long rope, and it gave Leo enough freedom to be herself, gave her enough distance to see sides of Sister St. Paul she'd been too close to see before: that side that seemed to understand and get along with the older girls; that side that liked to pray by herself in the chapel or outdoors by the shrine on the common; that side that could, on occasion, laugh.

After ditching her box in the bathroom, Leo went into the lab to give the rabbits the wilted lettuce in her pocket. The rabbits had been on her mind a lot lately. She was worried that without Calsa around during the summer, no one would pay any attention to them--over Easter vacation Snookems had died.

"I wish I could take you home with me," she told Ringo as he nibbled on her fingers. "Just think, in nine more days I'll wake up in my own bed every morning. And get something to eat anytime I want.

And go to the bathroom without raising my hand. Just nine more days and I won't have to do no more chores, or go to mass every day, or hear Doris say how fat she is, or listen to that friggin' bell . . . Too bad you can't come with me."

She stroked the rabbit, thinking of home, wondering if her father had opened that bottle yet. All during vacation she'd watched for the signs, had waited for him to tangle his words, for that familiar scent on his breath to return. It hadn't happened. But the house had started to whisper again, just like it had last summer, and somehow she knew it was only a matter of time. It was the way he had said "just in case." More than anything she hoped she was wrong, that he would continue to stay sober, that he would keep that bottle in the drawer like Jack's father kept his cigarettes on the shelf. But if he didn't . . . well, as Memere liked to say, she'd cross that bridge when she came to it.

"At least he ain't as bad as Huck's father," Leo told the rabbit. "Huck's didn't even love him."

Just then, Calsa walked in whistling like a siren. "Better find a good place to hide. St. Paul just tripped over your box in the bathroom and she's rippin'."

Leo smiled, then laughed. "That box runs her over even when I ain't around."

That evening the underclassmen were allowed

into the gym an hour before the prom to see what it looked like. Walking across the light layer of sawdust on the gym floor, Leo looked around in wonder. The place where she played basketball had been transformed. The ceiling was camouflaged with twisted royal blue streamers and hanging tinfoil stars. Fake palm trees and beds of tissue paper flowers were planted on the walls and small card tables with white cloths and flickering candles were stationed around a dance floor. Above the stage a sign sparkled the prom's theme--No Man Is An Island.

Later, as she and the others in her dorm watched the seniors walk across the courtyard with their dates, she felt as though the evening air was touched with magic. Dressed in soft shades of lilac, blues, and pinks, their hair piled in curls on top of their heads, the seniors had been transformed into princesses. And she found herself wishing that she, too, were about to enter that fairyland with its stars and streamers. She would wear a long white dress with flowers in her hair, and Jack would wear a black tux like those other boys, and maybe, as they danced under the silver stars, he would give her a girlfriend-boyfriend kiss.

On Sunday the seniors graduated and left with their parents after tearful good-byes. On Monday, Leo headed toward their rooms with her box out of habit.

"Wow," she said, entering the first room, which had been Stella's.

Everything was gone: the flowered trash can, posters, family pictures; the purple bedspread, curtains, scatter rug; the clutter of toiletries and nicknacks from the bureau; the books, photo albums, and horse statues from the shelves.

She sat down on the bed's bare mattress. Stripped of Stella, the room seemed so much bigger, the walls so naked. There has to be something left of her, thought Leo. She got up and checked the bureau drawers, the closet, under the bed, and found nothing. Abandoning her box, she went into the other rooms, searching them in the same way, carefully looking for traces of the seniors that had lived there--Tina, Gail, Doris . . .

After a thorough inspection she was still empty-handed--not even a candybar wrapper in Doris's room. It bothered her, made her think of Hope's alcove: how easily lives were erased. Despite the warm sun coming through the windows, it felt like winter.

Later that day, when no one was around, she borrowed a hammer and a few nails from Sister Rita's toolbox. She squirreled them outside, and sneaked around the building to the back bulkhead. There, hidden from view, she went to work on one of the bricks.

Being the last week of school, there were no study halls, and as the other girls lounged in the rec hall, or sat at the snack bar, or sunned themselves in the chairs on the porch, Leo was diligently chipping away. Red dust collected under her fingernails and flecks of brick speckled her hands. A callused blister grew between her fingers as she painstakingly chiseled each letter with a nail. When she was finally finished with the carving, she took a black pen and ran it along the groves of each letter, tracing them over and over, embedding the ink into the brick.

Wiping sweat from her forehead, she stood back and admired her work. Unless someone was looking for it or happened upon it by accident, the inscription chiseled into that one small brick was hard to notice against the huge brick wall. Still she was satisfied, certain her message would remain for a long, long, time: *Leo Was Here!*

As Leo sat alone in the rec hall, waiting for the supper bell to ring, she decided the place was too damn quiet without the seniors around. Cripe, she thought, I almost miss hearing Doris say how fat she is.

All week, everyone had walked around the school, looking like their dog had just died. No one had even written anything funny in her autograph book, except Calsa. It was all mushy stuff about how they'd miss her next year, and how the place wouldn't be the same without her getting into trouble all the time. She looked down at the open page,

Evette's message staring up at her: *I'll miss watching the news with you kid and I'll never forget The Pony Express! Free at Last! Free at last! A.F.A. Evette.*

Leo shut her autograph book, then ran her hand over the cover. Everyone was upstairs packing and bawling their eyes out--and what for? Tomorrow they were going home! And she was going home for good! After tomorrow, she'd be walking barefoot again and swimming at the pool. She stretched her legs as if she could already feel herself submerged in the water, arms stroking, eyes watching that good old black line.

She looked out at the courtyard, then beyond to the gym. She still hadn't figured out why someone would ever make a building that looked like a tuna can. There were a lot of things she hadn't figured out completely--like Hope, and the war, and her father's need to drink. As Huck said, "some things just don't make sense." But she'd hang onto to them, for though she didn't understand them now, she knew they were too important to forget.

"Leo, do you have your packing done?" asked Sister Theresa, as she walked into the room.

Leo swiveled in her chair. "You kidding? I was packed three weeks ago."

"I thought they might help your hands," Leo told Sister Alphonse after the nun unwrapped the rubber gloves Leo had bought with some of her Pony

Express money. "Wearing those, your hands won't get so chapped; won't get to bleeding like they sometimes do from all your scrubbing."

"Merci, Merci, best ting I ever get," said Sister Alphonse. "You good to think of old nun like me. I think of you, too. I give you dis."

"It's beautiful," said Leo, fingering the St. Christopher's medal. "I'll never take it off except when I'm swimming."

Sister Alphonse smiled and nodded her head. "Father blessed it. It keep you safe."

Leo looked down at her empty box that stood beside the incinerator and felt her throat tighten. She and Sister Alphonse had just dumped the trash together for the last time.

"Father Richie, he love you, too." Sister Alphonse continued. "He say you a kind girl. I say hard worker! I will miss my Petite Chapeau. You the best one."

Leo slipped her arms around the little nun and gave her a hug. "So are you, Sister. So are you."

Leo and Angie sat side by side on the playground at St. Christopher's. Ten minutes before, the school had let out for the summer and now they were the only kids left in sight. As they'd waited for the privacy, Leo had felt awkward, as if she didn't know Angie at all. Even the schoolyard seemed different to her; the air too hot, the sky too blue.

Already she missed the sharp scent of coal on those gray winter mornings, and the icy feeling of her bare hands against the steel monkey bars. Already, she missed her friend.

"I got you a present," said Angie sheepishly. From her school-bag she pulled out a red baseball cap. "I know it ain't as nice as your other one, but look here, it says Fred's Hardware, South Benton, Maine . . . Thought it might make you think of me sometimes."

Leo took the hat and tried it on.

"Shit, it's too big," said Angie disappointed.

"It's great," Leo told her. "I'll grow into it. Hey, I've got something for you, too." From her bag she took out a present wrapped in tissue paper and handed it to Angie.

Angie carefully opened the gift, then held up the paperback, the sun reflecting off its shiny cover. "Gee thanks, Leo."

"I wanted to buy you one like Hope gave me, but I didn't have enough Pony Express money for a hard cover copy." Leo pointed with her finger. "That's Huckleberry Finn; that's Jim; and that's the raft they sailed down the Mississippi on. You know how I'm always talkin' about Huck, now you'll get to read all about him yourself."

"I can't wait," said Angie. "I'll start reading it as soon as I get home."

"Speaking of home," said Leo, standing up. "Memere will be here soon. I guess I better get going." She looked down at Angie whose chin was trembling, and it made Leo want to cry, too. She leaned over and hugged her, shyness melting under their embrace.

"I know I won't write," Angie sniffed.

"We can always call each other," said Leo, breaking their hug.

"But it's long distance to Portland. My mother wouldn't go for that."

"All you got to do is call collect. Use the pay phone at the pharmacy and your mother will never know."

"Boy you're always thinkin'," said Angie, writing down her number. "No wonder you got the best grade award."

"That's just 'cause there was nothing else for me to do but study over there," said Leo, as they exchanged numbers. "Next school, I'll probably get all F's again."

"It ain't gonna be any fun without you around next year," said Angie, hugging the book to her chest. "I'm gonna miss you bad."

"Don't get mushy on me, you'll make me puke." Leo looked across the schoolyard to the woods where they'd smoked their first cigarette. "Me too, you know? . . . Listen, I'd better go . . . I'll call you."

"No kidding?"

"No kidding."

Leo turned and walked up the path, looking back only once at her friend who was still sitting in the schoolyard.

"I've been looking all over for you; where've you been?"

Leo shut her locker door and looked at Maggie. "Memere here?"

"No," she just called. Said something went wrong with her hose. The guy fixed it, but she's just leaving Portland now."

"You mean her radiator hose?" asked Leo.

"I don't know what kind of hose. Do I work at a gas station?"

"Did she say the car overheated?"

"You hang around Hal too much." Maggie picked up her suitcase. "Aren't you going to come upstairs? Everyone's leaving."

"I'll be up in a minute," Leo told her. "I gotta say good-bye to the animals."

Maggie rolled her eyes. "You're really weird."

"So what?" said Leo, making a face at her. "And Sister Alphonse loved her gloves, too. Said it was the best present she ever got. So put that in your holy pipe and smoke it."

Maggie walked off, shaking her head in disgust. "A pair of rubber gloves. God, I'd bawl my eyes out."

Aw, what's Maggie know, thought Leo, she wants to come back here next year.

Afternoon sunlight bounced off the chrome sinks as Leo entered the lab. All the microscopes had been put away and the glassware covered with plastic bags. She went over to the cages, first saying good-bye to the rats and hamsters, then her favorites--the rabbits.

"Calsa's going to be back before you know it. She'll swipe treats for you, she promised me." Leo unlocked the first cage and let Ringo sniff her fingers before patting him. "You can't go and get sick again, Ringo, or they'll make you drink that yellow crap." She gave Ringo kisses, then moved on to George's cage. As soon as she opened the latch, he began hopping around in circles.

"Poor George, you'd loved to get out of here wouldn't you fella?" The rabbit twitched his ears as though agreeing. "That's right," Leo told him, smoothing back his fur, "God didn't make rabbits to live like this." Really, thought Leo, Adam and Eve didn't have no rabbits living in cages, and Jesus never had a pet bunny that she knew of. "No, God made you to hop in the grass, and eat clover anytime you want."

As Leo began to hum *Born Free*, the plan was already forming. The nuns wouldn't even miss them until tomorrow. And it wasn't as if she'd be stealing them; she just be moving them to where God wanted them to be in the first place--outside.

Ringo was heavy, but he didn't squirm as she crept down the back stairs and out the fire escape door. When she got to a shady area by the pond, she put him down gently. "There you go, Ringo. You're free!"

George didn't like to be held. He dug his back

feet into her arms as she carried him, battling for freedom the whole way. By the time she got to where Ringo was still sitting, her arms were covered with long red scratches.

"There you go. See, Ringo waited for you." George leapt from her arms and hopped off madly, stopping only for a second to sniff before bounding away again. Ringo still sat where she'd left him, as if he were frozen to the spot. She nudged him gently, but he only took one hop before freezing again.

"Go on Ringo. Don't you want to go with George?" She sat down and patted the rabbit and it hopped into her lap, hiding its head in the crook of her arm. "You don't want to go, do you fella? You're scared. I can feel you shaking all over."

She picked the rabbit up, then glanced around for George, spotting him near Sister Martha's garden. He'll be fine, she told herself, then returned to the school and put Ringo back in his cage.

Leo knocked softly on Sister St. Paul's door. "Can I come in?" she asked, stepping into the room.

Sister looked up from her desk. "You already are."

Leo's eyes skimmed the room. It was the first time she'd come in here on her own. "Memere's going to be here soon, and ah, I just wanted to give you something. I made a deal with God about it."

"That certainly sounds interesting, Leona," said the nun giving her a curious look. "What is it?"

"This." Leo pulled the item from her uniform pocket and placed it gently on Sister's desk. "I don't need it anymore."

The nun reached for the visor with hesitating fingers, then her hand recoiled. She stood up and, turning her back on Leo, walked to the window. "I might have made some mistakes, Leona. But I want you to know, I always had your best interest in mind."

She watched the nun carefully. Sister's voice had sounded like she might cry. "That's okay, Sister. Memere says it's all right to make mistakes. She says that's how people learn."

"Your grandmother is a smart woman."

"I know," said Leo. "No one can beat her at cribbage."

Sister turned around, a slight smile on her flushed face. "I told your mother we would consider taking you back as a freshman, if you changed your ways."

Leo looked down at the long scratches on her arms: Ringo wanted to stay in a cage while George couldn't wait to get out. "I don't want to come back here, Sister St. Paul. And I'm not going to change-- I'm just going to get bigger."

"I'll pray that you do both."

"See you later, Sister."

"Good-bye, Leo . . . God be with you."

"He always is," said Leo with a smile, then turned and left Sister St. Paul's office for the last time.

The car was hot, Maggie was bawling, and Leo's legs were already sticking to the upholstery. As Memere drove the red Volkswagen down the driveway, Leo looked back at the school with its brick walls and narrow windows, feeling just a twinge of sadness. Somehow she knew she was leaving behind something more than her visor or her name on that brick, yet she wasn't quite sure what it was. She pressed her face against the window and, for a split second, thought she saw something white move near Sister Martha's garden. "Bye, George."

"What was that, Leo?" asked Memere.

"Ah nothin'," said Leo. "Just saying good-bye to a friend."

THE END

Y
Dea
    Deans, Sis
Brick Walls

		DATE DUE		
AUG 1 2 2002				